PENGUIN BOOKS

THE AMERICAN DREAM

Alice Huang Wijaya (黄于庭) is a Chinese Indonesian writer, multimedia storyteller, and tech professional currently based in Singapore.

She has studied, worked, and travelled extensively in the United States, Europe, and Asia throughout her twenties. A versatile multimedia storyteller, she covers a wide variety of eclectic topics such as sex, gender and relationship, underground culture, psychedelics, and spirituality, technology, cryptocurrency and finance. Her work has appeared for media publications like *VICE, Rice Media, Cointelegraph,* and *The Edge Media Group.*

The excerpts of her debut autofiction *The American Dream* had been workshopped during her studies with esteemed writers such as Laura Van Den Berg and Jamaica Kincaid. It was also shortlisted for SingLit Station 2020 Manuscript Bootcamp award. Alice holds a Bachelor of Arts from Harvard University.

T0001737

Advance Praise for *The American Dream*

'I am touched. How someone managed to capture the complexity of sex work in these few pages astounds me. I felt for everyone and no one, I fell in love and in hate. You walked me through the intimate turns and confusion that are innate to a job so entrenched in human emotion and vulnerability. I am made to think about why power is structured the way that it is—and to be lost in that enthrall of power at the same time.'

—Eva Oh, award-winning international dominatrix
and former escort, Sex Worker of The Year 2022 at
German Fetish Ball

'From a later, more knowing place, the narrator steers us seamlessly between tales: the story of the rich man's suicide pact, taking place over the course of a fateful spring break week; the story of Cassie's time at Harvard and her relationship with the "magnetic" Zaneta; and the story of Cassie as a child whose parents "never held hands", combing through the detritus of a marriage for evidence of love. The stories entrance as they unsettle, asking questions about love and worth that weigh on the mind long after the mesmerizing read is over. This bizarre and vivid story will do well in cinematic rendition!'

—Shao Wei Chew Chia, Harvard College alumni, author of
The Rock and The Bird (2013), winner of The Royal
Commonwealth Society Essay Competition and
Hedwig Anuar Children's Book Award 2015

'Get ready for a trip, Alice has one of the most magnetic voices you'll ever encounter.'

—Nicholas B. Chua, HarperCollins' Author Academy alumni,
writer, editor and booktoker at @kaikaku_

'The *American Dream* is a stunning one-of-a-kind debut. It's irreverent, subversive, often shocking, but I could not put it down. Peel back the layers underneath the caper set-up and there's a moving, astute story of self-discovery, reaching into the past to trace Cassie's journey from a convent school in Indonesia to Harvard. Throughout, Huang Wijaya's writing is propulsive, provocative and absolutely captivating—she brings to life the sheer neurosis of Harvard life and the coming-of-age confusion we all face on the cusp of adulthood. I can't wait to see what's next from her.'

—Selina Xu, Harvard College alumni,
Bloomberg journalist and blogger at selinaxu.com

'Bold, vibrant and incisive, Huang Wijaya's autobiographical novel is a breath of fresh air in its approach to difficult topics from which a lesser author may shy away. While cutting at times, its narrative voice is unapologetic and deeply authentic, keeping the reader riveted throughout; it promises to take you on an exhilarating adventure through the weird and the wonderful.'

—Joelle David, Literary Art Curator, creator of 2022
Art x Poetry Exhibition : A Journey Down The Singapore River

'The *American Dream* is an exploration into the depths of human relationships, ethical dilemmas, and the ramifications of the decisions we make.

And though the subject may prove to be challenging for certain readers, The *American Dream* is a stoic reminder of the importance of the choices we make and the impact they have on both ourselves and those we exist with.

There's power in the faculty of choice in shaping our destinies, and The *American Dream* warmly—and cordially—invites us to explore the nuances of that human experience.'

—Zat Astha, Editor and investigative
journalist for *The Peak*, previously *Rice Media*

The American Dream

Alice Huang Wijaya

PENGUIN BOOKS

An imprint of Penguin Random House

PENGUIN BOOKS

USA | Canada | UK | Ireland | Australia
New Zealand | India | South Africa | China | Southeast Asia

Penguin Books is part of the Penguin Random House group of companies
whose addresses can be found at global.penguinrandomhouse.com

Published by Penguin Random House SEA Pvt. Ltd
9, Changi South Street 3, Level 08-01,
Singapore 486361

First published in Penguin Books by Penguin Random House SEA 2023
Copyright © Alice Huang Wijaya 2023

ISBN 9789815058079

Typeset in Garamond by MAP Systems, Bangalore, India

www.penguin.sg

For my parents.
Thank you for never giving up on each other.

Contents

Chapter One

The Suicide Pact of The Very Rich Man

'We are going to help him die, Cassie,' Zaneta told me that afternoon, over steaming cups of soy milk latte, as casually as if announcing a gardening project.

'How?'

I shifted uncomfortably in my seat, looking around. Zaneta had briefed me several times to prepare me for this meeting, yet I could not help feeling caught off guard. The student centre was buzzing with people, chatting animatedly over plates of salad and cups of coffee, laptops propped open. Bright rays of sunshine poured through the clear glass walls, making yellow rectangular patches on the wooden panelled floors. Spring had arrived cheery and bright, smiling eagerly over the last inches of melting frost.

'Well, we don't know yet. But the details can be figured out slowly when the time comes . . . I am thinking . . . something along the lines of carbon monoxide poisoning . . . Something simple.' She flicked her Shirley Temple curls. Today I saw streaks of pink and green in them. 'Come on, it's going to be great. He is loaded.'

I shook my head in disbelief. 'How did you even find this guy?'

'Wrong question. He found me.'

She smiled at me with perfect white teeth. Her hair, bleached in peroxide blonde, shone like the sun. Her olive skin glowed satin mix of cutting-edge buzzwords, 'So this blockchain integrated ledger right here, we are devising new ways to incorporate it into the end-to-end user agreement . . .'

'How was that AI conference last week, did you get to meet with the venture capital rep . . .'

'My lab, we are working with Professor so-and-so and Professor so-and-so, right now in the process of testing CRISPR application to lengthen telomeres in mice . . .'

'So guess what, I just got a callback from both McKinsey and Bain, they wanted to fly me to New York over the break . . .'

A pair of ethnic Indian students claimed the table next to us and started chatting about medical school applications. One of them had an extremely loud and nasally voice. 'No, no, Vimal, listen to me. You've got to leverage your network here, get at least three referrals . . . What's that? No, no I think your MCAT is fine . . . but sure, go ahead and retake it later this year. I personally took it thrice, even though I didn't really need to.'

Zaneta rolled her eyes at them, positively unimpressed.

'How much . . . ahem . . . how much are we talking about here?' I lowered my voice, gingerly, while Vimal's friend crescendoed into a deafening laughter.

Zaneta had to take a moment to think. 'Oh well . . . I don't have an exact number for you . . . but maybe four to five . . .? Of course, I'll get double that . . . it's only fair. He also has properties you know . . . one in Florida, one in LA, one in Palm Springs, one in New York, I'm down to split them equally.'

'Four to five . . . million?' My voice trailed off to a whisper. At this point, the Indian mentor sounded like he was yelling right into my ears. 'PERSONALLY, I ENJOYED MY ROTATION ACROSS THE COUNTRY, THAT WAS HOW I MATCHED WITH MY RESIDENCY PROGRAM UPSTATE . . . WONDERFUL GROUP OF PEOPLE . . . FIND A FEW MENTORS YOU CAN TRUST.'

'Yes. Million. US Dollar.' Zaneta held my gaze. 'He is seventy-six. No kids, no immediate family members left, he's got one younger brother he is not on any speaking terms with.'

I felt weak in the knees, even though I was sitting down. A well-paid general doctor who saved fifty per cent of his annual income would need up to twenty years to accumulate five million, discounting paying off mounting student loans and whatnot. Truth is that most of the world would never live to see that much money in their savings accounts.

'In the spring break, he can fly you down to Florida, see each other, feel each other out. Ten grand for the initial meet-up, no expectation whatsoever. You can certainly decide after that. Are you in?'

I took the last swig of my latte so quickly that it burnt my throat. 'Has he . . . has he seen my profile yet?' I had put up a picture of myself in a low-cut dress during a friend's wedding. In the picture, my cleavage was visible, and my face appeared darkened, save for the bright red lipstick I was wearing for the occasion. Chin tilted, lips pouting, gaze mysterious and inviting, I practiced that selfie for at least a dozen times.

'We won't be having this conversation if he hasn't.'

'Don't you think—that—that I will be a letdown?' I touched my dark hair, brittle and puffy in all the wrong ways. 'I mean, compared to you.'

She laughed in a way that always made me think of Christmas bells on a moving sleigh. 'Oh shut up, stop comparing. You are more than a decade younger than I am. They like us young you know, in case you haven't figured it out. All you need to do is be yourself. You are more than enough. Trust me.'

I bit my lower lip. The proposal sounded insane, I could already envision so many grounds for potential arrest . . . but hey, at the very least, I would be escaping this chilly spring weather to bask on Florida's sunny beaches. I had missed the ocean like crazy.

'APPLY TO ALL OF THEM, ALL OF THEM. AS LONG
AS YOU GET INTO ONE, YOU'LL BE ALL SET. LUCKILY,
I GOT INTO THIS MEDICAL SCHOOL … I MEAN, IT'S
LIKE HITTING A JACKPOT . . .'
That did it.
'Alright. Count me in.'

America was a gift in the mail. An April Fool's surprise gift of
reality. I checked my inbox to read those words 'Congratulations,
you have been selected from the pool of academically talented . . .'
From the pool of academically talented . . . such grand words
of validation, such blessed approval. Everything afterwards was
a whirlwind of congratulations and praises. All my friends and
enemies, far and close, acknowledged that I had landed myself a
once-in-a-lifetime deal to study in one of the best universities in
the world. Everybody was proud, jealous, excited. I had hundreds
of likes on social media, on top of a gazillion new friend requests.
A surprise gift in the mail. A four-years' worth of time bomb
ticking in the mail. Little did I know that by the end of the gift
there was an explosion, and it was a binary either/or—Either it
propelled you to reach the stars of your dream, or made you fall
from grace and burn in hell.
When I first stepped my feet on the hallowed grounds of
Harvard University, I thought to myself of all the world-famous,
all the venerable leaders-inventors-entrepreneurs-artists-scholars-
presidents and so on, who had both stepped on the same grass,
loitered about the same student halls, ate from the same silverware.
Nobody had ever gotten over this place, nobody. Everyone was
in awe of everything and everything that had ever happened here,
even more than when they were the students themselves.

My dormitory, Thayer Hall, was the most convenient hall of all the freshman dormitories. It was humongous, located at the middle of the campus yard and running horizontally all the way to the end of the campus. At one end, it pointed directly to the science department building and the stately dining hall, where food was served to all freshmen. At the other end, it led to the main lecture hall, where most academic classes took place. My room was underneath a charmingly slanted wooden roof with a skylight. I had a quiet South Korean roommate who had her eyes on the finance industry since the first day of school. Besides attending classes and finance and consulting groups, she mostly ate Korean instant noodles in front of her laptop, watching K-Pop dramas.

I walked around wide-eyed, appreciating all the libraries, dormitories, and function halls. These red-brick buildings brimming with historical grandeur, most of which would allow me access via a scan of my precious student card. The yard was old, the grassy patch looked like somebody went over it to pluck and bulldoze parts of it at will, leaving behind an ugly, balding yard. The few trees that lined the perimetre of it appeared to be saving graces. Colourful plastic chairs were littered around with first-year students sitting on them smiling self-contented expressions, some accompanied by their family members.

The weather was chilly and crisp. Leaves turned golden before my eyes, like a fairy tale spread that creaked underneath my footsteps. The first signs of snow came early in October. I licked my first snowfall on the tip of my tongue. It tasted cold and tangy. The air stung my nose as I breathed it in, but I could not have been happier to embrace fall and the coming of winter.

I quickly declared anthropology as my major, thinking of overseas travel opportunities that I would be privy to, exotic places and exotic people, and life Experience with capital E.

I joined the theatre troupe, the ballroom dance team, and a few school publications. I made friends, attended classes, and ate in the big dining hall with a buffet spread that was almost too much to handle. I went on weekend trips to hike in the mountains with different student groups.

Sometime in early December, just as the first semester of classes concluded, Zaneta came into my life.

I was working on a final paper when I heard loud, incessant rapping at my door. I opened it to the whole board members of the theatre troupe grinning at me, looking inebriated. 'Surprise visit for Cassandra, rookie number 005,' a blonde girl announced. I knew her as Beverly, the social committee chair, an all-American smiling beauty from North Carolina. She was carrying a red plastic solo cup.

'Whoa! Guys . . . What is this?'

'Your initiation, sweetheart,' Greg, an auburn-haired Biology senior, shoved a half-full red solo cup into my hand. 'Drink up.' It was pure vodka.

I had heard rumours of midnight surprise visits and hazing among different student groups, but I never expected a bunch of nerdy theatre lovers who quoted Shakespeare and Meisner in casual conversations would pull off anything unusual. Yet, even as a freshman, I understood that the necessity to prove one was a wild party animal, on top of being bookish and accomplished, was an unspoken college requirement. If you wanted to climb to the top of the college ladder, you had to present yourself as a reckless academic.

I downed the cheap vodka in one big gulp, and everybody applauded. My cheeks warmed up in an instant. I let them grab my arm and lead me to the John Harvard statue in the middle of the yard, just a short walk from my dormitory. It was rumoured that drunk college students peed on that statue on a nightly basis. This ridiculous rite of passage was set along a few other enduring traditions—running naked across campus on finals night and having sexual intercourse in the Widener Library's stacks.

'It's about time you pee on that statue, Cassie,' said Stéphane solemnly, a lithe French-Canadian-Haitian who harboured serious ambitions to be the president of Haiti one day. 'It's a small third-world country constantly racked by earthquakes, there is barely any competition!' He grinned a mouthful of white teeth from ear to ear. 'Peeing on John Harvard has been an initiation rite of passage for all members of our esteemed theatre troupe since 1978. All of us here tonight had done it, except for you.'

I had to be a reckless academic. I had no other choice.

The seniors hoisted me up the pedestal. I looked at stinking yellow pee that pooled over the base of the statue, dripping down to patches of balding grass below. I could not believe my senses. The rumour was true after all. It was difficult for me to find a nice dry spot amidst the pool of urine. When I finally did, I watched my right shoelaces fall limply into the yellow goo next to the shoe. It was disgusting.

'This is disgusting!' I yelled at them. They cheered.

I unzipped my pants and pulled them down to my knee. The sharp cold air quickly bit my naked skin, making my teeth chatter. As I squatted down and reached at my underwear, a loud police siren wailed behind my back. From the corner of my eyes, I saw the Harvard University Police Department car sailed across the yard to where we were stationed. Caught red-handed. Peeing on the statue. I froze midway, squatting, helpless.

'Ma'am, please keep your pants on,' a crackling, static voice blared from the car's radio speaker. 'Keep your pants on, I repeat, keep your pants on.'

'Hurry Cassie, we gotta go!' Stéphane implored.

I pulled up my pants, zipped them in one hasty gesture, and jumped to the ground, rolling headfirst. The rest of the theatre troupe scrambled and fled in every direction as a police officer

'I . . . I . . . I have . . .' I was thinking of the final paper halfway done in my laptop up in my tiny dorm room, yet even as I willed myself to remember the thesis statement, I could not take my eyes off this strange and fantastic girl, admiring every inch and angle of her profile. I shook my head. 'Sure, I'd love to come. I have never seen a drag queen in my life before.' I offered my hand, 'I am Cassie by the way. What's your name?'

When she smiled, her whole face lit up. It was magnetic. She took my hand.

'Zaneta. Pleasure to meet.'

Chapter Two

Florida Dreamin'

The plane landed on the tarmac of Palm Beach International Airport, ten minutes to ten. It was pitch black outside, save for several yellow lights at the periphery of the landing strip. My phone vibrated with Zaneta's message. *Hey hun, where are you? Covert is tired, he was so excited just now, he wanted to pick you up and show off his Jaguar, but now he is all sleepy . . .*

That's fine, but how am I supposed to get there? I replied. *I just landed.*

My phone vibrated again. *We sent Ali to pick you up. Wait at the taxi stand. He has your number, he'll call you if he can't locate you.*

I stretch my arms above my head, it has been a tiring day. Spring break had finally arrived. After taking my Chinese literature midterm exam in the morning, I ran straight to the Harvard Square T station, rolling my small luggage through uneven pebbled sidewalks, then through sticky train compartments, then across carpeted airport halls that went on forever. I made it to the domestic flight boarding area just barely in time. Covert flew me first class, so I had all the legroom I needed. Yet, despite the infinite champagne refills and free in-flight movies, I was unable to relax for the whole three hours flight.

I had never considered sugar dating a possibility before. I was not someone who had that kind of effect on men, someone who flirted and batted her eyelashes. Growing up,

I was always the sensible one, the quiet one. I had only one decent boyfriend in my life—a piano-playing, dimpled-smiling boy back when I attended a boarding school in Singapore. It was a lukewarm relationship, and it ended because I had to move abroad. He did not beg me to continue long distance. I did not press further.

Zaneta told me to create a profile on Strings Attached when she first called me about the arrangement. 'Why don't you put up some nice pictures and a few descriptions about yourself and I'll show them to Covert. I'll get in touch once he gives me the green light.'

Already, my inbox was brimming with messages from different men with cringe-worthy profile names—BigDaddy236 and MasterDom888 and IAmYourKing4Eva. I spent the past week talking to them and exchanging more pictures, out of curiosity.

I had expected these men to be ugly and fat—indeed some of them were. Though there were plenty who looked attractive too, men in their thirties or forties, whom I would most likely swipe right on any other dating application. Most of them had too much money to burn, too little time to get a real girlfriend, and too many barriers to cultivating real intimacy.

'Look, the time I'd have spent talking nonsense to a gazillion of girls through dating apps could have been used to earn good money to get an attractive, college-aged sugar baby,' a thirty-five-year-old neurosurgeon told me. 'I am a practical man. I know what I want. Money makes it straightforward and fair for both parties.'

There were also some who desired a real relationship. There were some who were cheating on their wives. There were some rich young high schoolers, who had zero confidence to approach a girl, yet unlimited pocket money from their parents. There were all sorts of people, all sorts of wants and needs, limitless configuration of arrangements.

There was an unmistakable electric thrill that went up and down my spine when I started discussing prices and logistics with these men. How much for a coffee date? How about a night over? Do I prefer a hotel room, what kind, with a fireplace, with a hot tub? Have I seen the Bermudas, would I like to go for a weekend? How about Paris?

I discovered that just by virtue of my age and gender, I could earn up to five hundred dollars sitting in a coffee shop chatting for a couple of hours. The bidder was a stout French businessman who travelled weekly from Paris to Boston. He had a huge Jewish nose and a pair of hooded, leery eyes that reminded me of the evil bishop character in Disney's animated *Beauty and The Beast*. It was interesting to find a real-life match for those exaggerated cartoon shapes, years after they were etched into my formative childhood brain. Back then, there was no question that I would end up with the golden Prince Charming, but now I understood that there was more surplus of Gastons and evil bishops than there were Princes in the world. If I were to be made into a cartoon character, perhaps I would end up as one of the talking furnitures.

I started seeing things differently in the mirror. My eyes, black and almond-shaped, took on a new glow of a pair of black pearls. Round button nose and melancholic lips now seemed almost adorable. I always thought my colouring fit into the background of things, but who knew the background of things also carried a price tag? If I were to tilt my chin up a little, gaze more provocatively, and pull my shoulders back, I would look like a different person. I walked around campus with a little bit more of a swagger. These small fingers with hanging cuticles, how much were they? Was lipsticked mouth priced higher than a plain one? If my body was sellable, then I could easily rearrange parts to fit into the most desirable mold. They were separate from me, they were manipulable, mutable, pliable.

Was it not Zaneta who told me that being a woman was both a gift and a curse? 'Honey, we run the world, all along it was us. However, we can never, never let it be obvious. Men must think they are the ones in control. Watch.'

We were walking downtown on Park Street. She smiled brilliantly at a passing man in a long coat. He stopped and asked to buy her coffee. She gave him her number instead.

'See, I let him call me, so then I would be able to call the shots where he should take me. Not coffee, but maybe a fancy dinner,' she told me later.

I did not really understand what she meant by all this. No matter what he ended up buying her, he was the one with the capacity to buy things.

Zaneta was always filled with ideas—the latest ploy to get rich, the latest exploration into the world of *avant-garde* sexual practices, the latest mischief and adventure, all proposed and checked off like a bucket list, just to get unusual kicks out of life. She was not one to be confined into the normal corporate rat race, she would rather die than sequester herself into a predictable cubicle life.

She saw me as a protégé, someone she took under her wings, someone she came to trust as a confidant, someone who understood, and even admired her unusual pursuits in life.

She never gave me a straight story of her past, it was checkered and strange, often sounding more like a fairy tale. She would pluck parts of it for anecdotes whenever she launched into one of her inspiring pep talks, but these parts changed on a whim, depending on what kind of advice she was preaching at that moment.

When she raved about the purity of romantic love, she recalled her childhood living in a convent in Israel, and how she never knew sex until her mid-twenties, when she gave her virginity to a long-standing high school sweetheart. Other times she proclaimed the gospel of body positivity and shared her journey battling anorexia while training to be Miss Fitness of Israel, how she was lost and then found, and moved to the United States of America to pursue nobler dreams. However, at some other times, when preaching about material versus spiritual wealth, she told stories about how she grew up cleaning houses for wealthy oil barons in Tel Aviv, and how no one had seemed to be genuinely happy with so much wealth.

'So, which one is it? Were you a maid or were you a nun? Did you really become Miss Fitness of Israel? How did you afford to come to America?'

She reached out and tousled my hair fondly.

I was never sure who she was, but that was part of her attraction.

With her, I felt free and infinite. She gave me a lot of space, in and out of myself, and as I stretched and expanded, I realized there was always room for more. The options of what I could achieve suddenly became limitless and the only thing that prevented me from being all that I could ever be, was myself. No one else mattered.

'Honey, you can be anyone you want to be. Look at me, I have done so much shit outside the boundaries of everyday people's comfort zone, that I simply have no room to judge others,' she always said with a flourish. 'Except maybe a murderer, you know, killing people with evil intent.'

She took me to a nudist retreat once, in an outdoor camp in The Hamptons. It was a gathering of white American hippie-types with strong ties to the flower children of the sixties. They liked to get together naked, engaging in polyamorous consensual sex, moonlight seances and skinny dipping into the ocean in the middle of the night. Many of them lived off trust funds or did random odd jobs like selling marijuana or practicing massage therapy.

I remembered going into the spa cabin with her, relaxing in the hot tub, flesh upon flesh, with other descendants of the flower children. There, people looked you right in the eyes, unperturbed by displays of uncovered nipples and penises. 'This is a place for ultimate body positivity,' said Anthony Robertson, one of the founders of the nudist community. Rumour had it that he was born in a commune and that his parents were hippies far more outrageous than he was. 'We see past bodies, colours, beliefs, orientations. We are one and the same. We are free, we are humans.'

Anthony had long coarse brown hair, a full moustache and a beard. He looked like Jesus with flower garlands in his hair. He had a long torso, long arms and legs, and a long penis. He booked the campgrounds once a year and arranged a retreat for three days and two nights, inviting everybody with 'positive energy' on his radar. It was unclear what he did for a living.

'You should stop being so concerned with the origin of things,' said Zaneta. 'The universe is a mosaic of colours, intermingling in a complex spider web of things, with connections that overlap each other in the most illogical and serendipitous way possible. Not everything is clear cut you know—childhood, school, work, business, family, yada yada yada . . . Many of us are not so straightforward.'

'I'm just curious, that's all. People's histories intrigue me.'

'Sometimes people just want to be . . . without many questions asked,' she said, as if signalling about my questioning into her past. 'The key to happiness is . . . just be, just being in the moment.'

In these communities, rarely would someone initiate the usual inquisitive exchanges—where are you from, what do you do for a living, how many siblings do you have? They would ask these— what's your favourite colour today, if you were an animal what would you be? How do you feel today, do you need a hug? And they would hug me, no further question asked.

We went skinny dipping in the ocean when it was high tide and dangerous. The sea rushed into the beach and receded again, rumbling and splashing, a gentle, giant monster lapping under the white moon. Its vastness engulfed me from within, opening a world of possibilities. My skin tingled from the salt—I closed my eyes and went under, it was all darkness, darkness so cold and so complete, so all-encompassing, a universe of its own. I thought of all the mythical creatures, the sea demons and gods and goddesses our imagination had come up with to compensate for its magnificent powers.

One of my wishful thinkings was to die in the ocean—to walk into a rising high tide one day and never return. There would be no remains of me, I would return to the ocean, merging with demons and gods and goddesses, with the white moon shining, guiding a safe passage of my departure. I would be back home at last.

The night was windy and warm. I waited at the airport's taxi pick-up stand, fingers curled around my luggage handle. I saw stretches and stretches of asphalt highways lined with thick palm trees, and glimmering rectangular buildings in the distance, everything awash with the yellow and orange glow from the streetlights. Buildings seemed to be flatter and shorter, things and objects more spread out here than they were in Boston. I can almost make out the sound of the ocean, somewhere in the background of cars wheezing past and palm fronds rustling loudly in the wind.

Ali came to pick me in a sleek long limousine. He is a youngish, middle-eastern, man, wearing a black uniform and white gloves. He rolled down the shotgun seat window and called out, 'Cassandra? Mr C sent for you. I am Ali.' I nodded and walked towards the limousine. He came out, heaved my luggage into the trunk and opened the passenger seat door for me in one smooth, trained motion. I climbed onto the red leather seats that smelled brand new.

'This is a little bit excessive, isn't it,' I murmured, almost to myself, as the limo sped along the highway.

'Mr C still has a year's subscription left with our company, ten rides per month. He barely uses it himself these days.' Ali looked into the rearview mirror. 'Are you a new girl?'

'I suppose you can say so. How many have you been sent to pick up?'

Ali shrugged. 'Not many, as far as I can tell. Maybe two, three, every six months or so? Plus Princess, of course. She comes regularly.'

'Princess? You mean Zaneta?'

'Is that her real name? She has curly blonde hair and very white teeth. She asked me to call her Princess.'

I could not help but let out a giggle. The more I thought about it, the more I realized how natural, how befitting, this job must be for Zaneta. She loved to be adored, to be worshiped on a pedestal. Sometimes she put on glittery butterfly wings and walked around downtown Boston just to attract passerby's attention.

'What accent is that from?' Ali asked. 'You are not American, are you?'

'I grew up in Indonesia until I was sixteen,' I told him. 'Then I attended a boarding school in Singapore. Then I moved here for university.'

'Indonesia! How exotic! I have always wanted to go to Bali,' he exclaimed. 'Just meditate by the beach, like *Eat, Pray, Love*, have you seen it?'

'Can't you meditate by the beach here?' I waved my hand in a general direction outside. 'Bali is overrated. There are a lot of traffic jams these days. Plastic trash all over the beach. Drunk, unemployed Australians bumming around.'

'Well that's true, that's true indeed,' Ali laughed. 'There are sharks here, I heard. I never really go to the beach here. Too busy with work. All day long, driving guests.'

'Where are you from, Ali?'

'Afghanistan. I came here seven years ago, I won the green card lottery. I first drove the buses, now I drive a limousine, next I might have my own car company.'

'Good for you.'

'How about you, after university, you'll work here?'

'I doubt so, no one seems to sponsor the H1-B. I only have one year to work.'

The H1-B was a notorious, long-term lottery work permit that cost thousands of dollars with only one-third chance of success. Most companies flat-out refused to sponsor H1-B for entry-level business and marketing roles, reserving their funds for precious engineering talent instead. The bulk of my job hunt this year consisted of receiving calls from potential employers repeating this grim reality over and over again—'We are sorry but our company policy does not sponsor the H1-B for this role, and we are looking for someone long term . . .'

Ali clucked his tongue sympathetically. 'Ah, I see. Yes, I heard it's tough these days. Especially now they have the anti-immigration president with that funny hair. Maybe you can find an American boyfriend to marry you, no?' He chuckles.

'Maybe. Maybe I will.' I looked outside the window again, streetlights and palm fronds smudged into orange–green blurs against velvety black. Truthfully, the idea of working day in day out logging some sales inventory on excel sheets, inside a steel-glass building downtown somewhere in America gave me heart palpitations, so I let out a tiny sigh of relief every time I received a rejection call.

The rest of the car journey passed in silence. Ali told me it was going to take another hour before we reached Mr C's apartment complex at Jensen Beach. I played a game of spotting neon franchise signs. Dunkin Donuts, Taco Bell, CVS, Walmart, Burger King, Starbucks. In this country, they kept the stores brightly lit past closing hours, all night long, every day, as if declaring to the world that they could afford it. 'What a waste of electricity,' my mother would say.

In Jakarta, we had a designated driver who drove us to a private Catholic school an hour and half away from home, back and forth, every other day that we were not taking the school bus. The driver slept all day long in the car while my sister and I sat through Mathematics, Science, Religion, Languages, and Social Studies classes. This meant we never had playdates after school, never ventured out to explore town for ourselves. There was home, there was the car ride, there was school, and there was home again. On the weekends, sometimes Mother and the driver took us to the air-conditioned malls, to watch the latest Hollywood blockbuster, shop for brand clothes, and eat restaurant food.

I spent almost all my childhood and early teenage years sitting down. I sat down in the car, in classes, in front of my desk doing homework, in my bed reading novels. When the piano teacher came, I sat down for a couple more painful hours stretching my short fingers over white-and-black keys. 'Hit one octave quicker! It says staccato!' barked the sullen piano teacher. He always wore a plaid shirt and formal black pants.

We had a live-in maid, named Siti, who came from a village in Central Java, and slept in a small room next to the washing machine. She had six fingers and six toes, on both hands and feet. The Javanese believed that this physical aberration brought misfortune, so no eligible bachelor would marry her. Her mother sent her to Jakarta to be a domestic helper. Everyday including on the weekends, she cleaned the whole house, did laundry, went grocery shopping and cooked three meals. I did not know how to sweep a broom or how to operate a washing machine until I was sixteen.

Father was often nowhere to be seen. For the longest time, he kept his business affairs under wraps. He slept all day long and went out at night and returned home in the morning smelling like roast duck, cigarette and alcohol. As far as I could tell, he entertained clients and guests and struck business deals in restaurants and karaoke parlours. Mother told me that these parlours were not the place for 'good, righteous women' like us. 'Only karaoke girls work there,' she said icily. 'They come from mainland China. Fresh off the boat.'

Once a month, burly tattooed men came to visit in the living room. They had dark skin, curly hair, and scars on their faces. Mother said they were Ambonese, an ethnic group from the eastern part of the country, and they were known to be strong and aggressive. When they came, we were expected to stay in our bedroom upstairs, so I never knew why they were there. Once, I sneaked outside and sat behind the balustrade of the staircase, eavesdropping. They talked to Father in hushed, raspy voices, so it was difficult to catch what they were saying. There were phrases—'players who did not pay', 'settling the score even', 'leave the rest to us.'

Mother spent most of her time watching soap operas and going to the salon, getting something done—hair, facials, nails. She went shopping for house supplies, supervised the maid, checked our homework, and went to fitness classes. During the day, whenever I was not in school, I often caught her lying face down on the mattress in the guest bedroom, blasting cheesy romantic pop songs at full volume. She stayed like that for hours at a time. She did not have any friends, because Father was not comfortable with her socializing outside without him. Sometimes they went to dinner or drinks together with their common friends, only sometimes. I rarely saw them engaging in anything beyond perfunctory routine dialogue. 'Honey, would you pass the soy sauce?' 'I need to settle the children's school fees by next week.' 'I notice we are out of toilet paper.'

I read a lot of foreign novels, and they inspired me to write stories. I tried writing fantastic kingdoms and orphans and magic and aliens like the stories I read, but they were always set somewhere else in the world outside, and I had zero access to that world. Hence, nothing I wrote felt real enough, just like how the outside world never felt real.

I switched strategy and started writing about my life, as I knew it.

This morning, I woke up at 6 a.m. as usual, because the mosque next door blasted the Arabic call for prayer through their outdoor speakers. I ate breakfast, two half-boiled eggs, and a glass of milk. I showered and brushed my teeth. I slept throughout the car ride to school. We had an assembly at the school yard as usual. Today was the red-and-white uniform day so I wore my white shirt with a red tie, and a red skirt. The first class was Mathematics, we learnt Pythagoras theorem. The second class was Biology, we learnt about photosynthesis. I ate two pieces of toast with butter and jam for the first recess. Then we had History class. We learnt about the 350 years of Dutch colonization over Indonesia. The next class was Religion, we read letters from John the Apostle. At lunch, I ate rice with fried chicken and pickled vegetables in the school cafeteria, and then went to the library to read Japanese comic books. After lunch we had Social Studies . . .

I stopped writing. This has got to be the most boring story of all time, I thought to myself.

When I first met Covert, I thought my mind was playing tricks on me. Zaneta walked him across the parking lot of a seaside apartment complex in Jensen Beach, where Ali dropped me off. The buildings looked old with paint walls peeling all over. The night continued to be windy, and I had to blink to get rid of the sand that got into my eyelids.

Covert was old, and tall and scraggly, like a tree creature bent and spent from the wrinkles of age. He sported a moustache, skin red and splotchy from the Floridan sun. He was certainly not one of those men who grew sophisticatedly handsome when they were older, he was just plain old and unattractive.

How could Zaneta possibly fuck him?—was the first question that came to mind. How could I possibly fuck him? Five grand over a spring break was good money, and I would loathe to see it go. Perhaps this was why she was so fond of inviting other girls over to entertain Covert. Instead of getting jealous, she probably felt a sense of relief, having not to be the only focus of the old man's sexual and romantic desires.

'Cassie, Cassie, sweetheart.' Covert opened his bony arms and kissed me on the cheeks. One, two, three. I shuddered, and I hoped it did not show. He wrapped his arms around my waist and directed me to the apartment building. Zaneta winked at me as we walked alongside each other.

'There are two bedrooms in the apartment. Is it okay if you sleep in Covert's room tonight?' Zaneta asked. I looked at her in horror, but she did not seem to get the signal.

'Where would you sleep?'

'The other room is mine.'

We rode an elevator up to the penthouse. The unit was huge and comfortable, though a little bit musty, with faded brown carpet and mirrors all over the wall. There was a marble-tiled kitchen by the door, with a marble kitchen island, a dining room, and a huge beige sofa in a living room that opened to a wraparound balcony overlooking the ocean. There were two bedrooms, one bigger, one smaller, and two bathrooms, one with a jacuzzi.

'We were just having a lovely seafood dinner, sweetie,' said Covert. 'I'll bring you tomorrow, we are going to dress up and eat at some fancy house club, the three of us, and Bonnie too!'

Zaneta told me later that Bonnie was a girl who lived two floors below, in an open relationship with her boyfriend. They just had a baby, and she was lactating. Covert paid to sleep with her, he particularly enjoyed sucking at her breast milk. I felt nauseous hearing this.

I nudged Zaneta to go into her room and closed the door behind me, while Covert rearranged things in his own bedroom to make space for me. 'I don't want to sleep with him tonight,' I told her, breathing in panic. 'I can't, I can't picture it.'

'Hey, hey, relax sweetie. You are not obliged to do anything.' Zaneta grabbed my face with both hands and looked deep into my eyes. 'Just sleep on the same bed with him, but you don't have to have sex with him today if you don't want to. Take your time, get comfortable first.'

'I don't know if I can ever get comfortable with him. I don't know if I can do this!' My voice rose one octave higher.

'Perhaps tomorrow after dinner, wine, and weed, you will be able to finally relax. Give it a chance. He has a beautiful cock, I promise,' Zaneta squeezed my shoulders. She had that smiling determined look in her eyes, the look she gave me every time she tried to convince me to do something outside of my comfort zone.

'Eyes on the prize honey. Eyes on the prize. Five million, think about it. You'll be all set to travel the world and write your novels.'

'You couldn't stand him, could you?'

She rolled her eyes. 'That's insane, hun. He is the loveliest gentleman alive, I promise.'

I opened the bedroom door and stepped outside. Covert was standing in the middle of the living room, his baseball cap askew on his head. His toothbrush moustache looked ridiculous on his splotched face. I smiled at him, yet I know that it came off more like a cringe.

'Hey sweetheart. Which side of the bed do you prefer?'

Chapter Three

Une Femme Fatale

I slept on the right side of the bed, inching towards the extreme edge of it, making sure I would not be in any physical contact with Covert by mistake. He seemed to be fast asleep the whole night, though he wiggled and moved about, his legs splayed diagonally across the bed, cornering me into a tiny vertical section at the periphery.

In the morning I woke up with his right hand on top of my chest. I turned to face him, and he looked at me cloudily. His breath hurried, with another hand he reached inside his boxers and stroked away.

I started screaming. 'Get off! GET OFF ME!'

Zaneta barged into the room. 'My sweethearts, what happened?'

'Nothing, nothing,' Covert quickly became flustered. 'Cassie here was just being shy and uncomfortable with a new person. It takes some time to get used to me.'

Zaneta gave me a look, then flashed her white sparkling smile. 'Well then, Cassie, would you like to have some breakfast now?'

I collected myself, and got off the bed, mumbling as I reached for my suitcase. 'Yes, some breakfast would be lovely. Let me change out of my pyjamas.'

On the table outside on the balcony, the breakfast spread featured eggs and toast, bacon and pancakes, juices and coffee. Zaneta expertly rolled and licked a joint and started lighting up. 'Baby, nothing beats getting high all day long by the beach,' she passed the joint in my direction.

I took a long drag and exhaled, the unmistakable loosening of muscles bit by bit spread through the back of my neck, my arms and shoulders.

Covert stepped outside, squinting against the rising sun. He touched my right shoulder. 'How are you feeling now?'

I shrugged his hand off and turned to pile some eggs and toast on a plate. 'Good, good. Please do sit, Covert. And eat something. This all looks so delicious!'

He pulled up a chair, sat down and straightened his legs over another chair, took the joint, stared into the distance. For a moment there was nothing but the sound of chewing and swallowing.

'Cassie, did you bring any bikini with you?' Zaneta pranced to the balcony, 'Get Covert to buy you a nice, lovely pair . . . then we can take some beautiful pictures by the ocean. Right, dear?'

Covert mumbled something about overpriced bikinis in the area, but Zaneta shrugged it off. 'Well, don't you think somebody as lovely as Cassie deserves the loveliest bikini in the world?'

I didn't even know if I wanted a pair of bikinis. I brought a full-body swimsuit, plain and practical. It sounded odd though, that someone who had a suicide deadline on his horizon would complain about overpriced swimwear.

Zaneta walked slowly towards me, leaned forward, and pressed her lips upon mine. They felt soft and electric. I closed my eyes, and my tongue reached for hers, she complied, and our lips danced in an embrace for about a minute or so. My whole body stiffened with anticipation, but my face and neck became very warm as if drinking wine.

She pulled away, looked at me and laughed. I felt an urge to pull her in and kiss her harder, but I remained motionless.

Covert let out a big sigh. 'Whew. That was hot!'

He told me to get ready, we were going bikini shopping.

Mother took us shopping most of the time, mostly on the weekends, when Father was busy catching up on his sleeping debt. She was a good spender, with an impeccable instinct for timeless styles at reasonable price points. I tended to mix and match eclectic things on a whim, plastic star bracelets with gold bangles, designer glasses she bought for me perched casually on my nose, my hair pulled up in a side ponytail.

'Don't be tacky,' she would say, and directed me to a Korean hair salon to get my bangs restyled. 'Invest in loose garments that fall in shape with your silhouette. Show a little bit of skin, not too much. What can be filled in with imagination is so much sexier than your open cleavage. Never, never go out without sunscreen.'

I was not sure where she got her knowledge from—she grew up in a small town in Sumatra, dropped out of her accounting degree to marry Father. She was merely twenty years old when they had my sister, before they moved to the capital, before Father launched his business.

'Guys are like butterflies, and we are the flowers. Let them roam about, they will return eventually for more nectar. Our job is to keep our crowns and colours healthy and bright,' she preached, and more, 'You have got to keep him interested. In whatever way you see fit.' I was perhaps too young to digest all these, but Mother was adamant that it was never too early to educate a girl on the Laws of Love—who should be loved and how much to love and why and how?

I never once questioned her wisdom. She was a dutiful mother, she did her best in ways that she knew how. Our underwear, neatly ironed, pressed, and folded like delicate napkins. Hot home cooked meals on the table for dinners. Our lunch boxes, filled with kaya and butter sandwiches, every day without fail.

There would be times though, when the air was dense in her black moods, buzzing imperceptibly like the calm before the storm. Her face flushed and frowned, as she went about sweeping and reordering, rearranging, scrubbing, soaping, folding, dusting and ironing, moping, washing, and wiping. She banned the maid from touching anything, busied around the house with such a determined efficiency until every speck of dust and every blob of dirt was removed from our squeaky-clean floors and walls. She would refuse to communicate, snapped at every little thing that came her way. When everything was done and dusted, she would lie in the guest bedroom and cry her eyes out.

I knew better to retreat at such moments, like a quiet mouse, careful not to take up more space than I already did. I buried myself behind my storybooks, even holding my breath when her sobs crescendoed into blubbering wails

My older sister, not so naturally sensitive, would sometimes play the piano at this moment, or turn on cartoon shows, and therefore she would bear the brunt of Mother's wrath. Mother slammed her bedroom door open and marched to the piano, whacked the back of her head with vengeance. 'What are you thinking, turning the volume up like that? Are you out of your mind?' And my sister would cry, her glasses askew on her nose from the force of her slap. She was cross-eyed, and the unevenness became even worse when she cried. 'Be quiet! I say, be quiet! You look even uglier than you already are when you cry like that!'

I once went about Mother's drawer and discovered her wedding album, cheaply printed photographs yellowing with time. She had big, curly hair—fashionable at the time. Her white dress ballooned ridiculously at her shoulders. I noticed a small bump, almost too small to notice if I weren't careful enough.

I wondered then, if Mother had felt trapped all this time, living a life that was not even her own choosing.

We drove to a swimwear shop along the dusty beach. Leggy blonde teenagers milling about with their splotchy lobster-red-skinned parents, trying out floral suits. I felt embarrassed; Covert was older than my father. He waited for me at the counter, wearing his sunglasses and cap, stubbled legs poking out of his trousers and ending in sneakers. I could be his adopted grandchild from China or a mail-order bride.

I grabbed a coral blue two-piece that seemed to be about my size and handed it to him. Covert grunted when he saw the price, it was around 150 dollars. 'Why are these frivolous things so expensive?' He took his wallet out and started counting the money in it.

'You don't have to buy them for me if you don't want to,' I said. 'It's Zaneta's idea anyway.'

He stopped midway, seemingly startled, and chuckled. 'No, no dear. Of course there is no problem at all. That's why you are here, to be pampered, remember?' He leaned closer and gave me a peck on my cheek. I was careful not to look at the young man behind the cashier. 'I am just complaining about The System, that's all . . . these companies . . . constantly ripping off tax-paying consumers!'

'Would you pay with credit . . . or cash?' the pimply teenager over the counter offered lazily. Covert grumbled into his pocket again, pulled out a wad of cash, and handed them to him. His eyes flit to the newspapers on the counter. The orange-coloured president with funny hair was waving at the front page, his barbie-doll platinum blonde wife smiling rigidly at his side. PRESIDENT VISITS PALM BEACH FOR A WEEKEND GETAWAY AT MAR-A-LAGO RESORT. 'What a coincidence,' Covert chuckled. 'And this First Lady of our nation—isn't she the most successful sugar baby in the world, eh? What do you think?'

The pimply teenager handed a note back to him, similarly lazy and unperturbed. 'Fifty bucks for your change, Sir.'

'Keep it,' Covert winked at him and took my hand fondly. There was no point hiding now. I squeezed his hand back.

'Can we get an ice cream now?' I heard myself saying, suddenly bolder. 'I feel like vanilla . . . maybe with Oreo crumbles.'

'Only if you promise to lick it very, very slowly.'

Was that an uncomfortable gaze I was sensing finally, the pimply teenager crumpling the fifty dollars note into his pocket? I stared at him, almost in defiance, before turning back to Covert. 'Oh I promise Daddy. I promise.'

* * *

We reached the apartment back just in time for lunch and headed to the beach to find Zaneta. I held a cone of vanilla ice cream, the gooey liquid swirls down my fingertips, making everything sticky and sweet. Zaneta was finishing her swim in the ocean. Beads of water in her platinum curls—a mermaid rising from the waves.

'Babes,' she said, 'Show me, show me your new hauls today!'

I shrugged, handing her the bag of bikini. She checked this out and clapped in delight. 'What pretty patterns! I love, *love* the flowers you've got there. This shade will be really great for your olive tones,' she pressed this against my skin. 'Would you like to put them on?'

'I don't feel like swimming,' I shaded my face against the sun, licking my ice cream slowly. I had stopped entertaining Covert and gone back to my usual defensive stance.

Covert leaned in to lick trickles of ice cream from my fingertips and smacked his lips in satisfaction. 'How about Bonnie—where is she now?'

'In the apartment upstairs sweetheart,' Zaneta wiped a bead of cream from his moustache endearingly. 'I see that you are craving for some milk ...'

'I do, I do indeed.'

I threw another glance of horror at Zaneta, but she seemed genuinely amused by this proposition. 'Well in that case, we can see what we can do today. Maybe we can play milk-sucking again, with a brand-new spectator Cassie.'

Okay, that does not sound too bad. I'd just have to watch.

'Here, check out my new pictures for Instagram,' she handed me her phone, open at the gallery. I scrolled through at least thirty well-lit pictures of her in colourful different bikinis and shawls, facing the crystal cool blue of the sea, in stark contrast with sparkling white sand dunes. 'Babe, these are gorgeous,' I smiled encouragingly. 'Who took these for you?'

She waved her hand dismissively, 'Just another old man passing by on the beach,' she shrugged, as if it weren't a big deal, because most often than not, it wasn't for her.

I looked at Zaneta with intent—if only I could write her down into pages and pages of words, exactly the way she spoke, the way she smiled, the way she tilted her head here and there. The way she lived a ridiculously free life. I was trapped by various insecurities, doubts, and too much care. Zaneta operated with a different frequency, and I wished I could get an access into her stream of thoughts, and imprint each into my own consciousness. I wished I could feel the same sense of entitlement, it was my belief that the universe would give you exactly what you thought you deserved, and however hard I tried to will that belief, deep inside I was still a fraud. I could not help it.

Zaneta passed the phone to Covert. 'Now sweetie, would you mind? I have juuust a few other pose ideas . . .'

I went back to the penthouse by myself, tasked with carrying Zaneta's overflowing beach bag. The door opened by a string of code—1875 and it blinked green. I had not had the chance to inspect the whole unit and I noticed that it looked bigger and brighter under the sunlight. Perhaps last night I was imagining dampness, because I was nervous, but now, I thought everything looked and smelled like how a luxury property should look like.

I noticed that the faded brown carpet was not exactly faded, it was intended to be lighter than the average brown colour. The furniture was not exactly old, they were supposed to be retro. I saw that the beige sofas were actually brand new, but their striped patterns made it look like the seventies. I noticed now, with appreciation, colourful pin-up prints on the wall, along with classic film posters such as *Pulp Fiction* and *Bonnie and Clyde*, and I suspected Zaneta might have put them up. The kitchen was fully equipped with sparkling appliances—glossy triple-door refrigerator, state-of-the-art oven that looked intimidating, elegant electric stove, blender, espresso machine, and various other apparatus I could not even name. The dining room had a full-sized table that sat five people. The floor-to-ceiling mirrors all over the walls brought an expanded illusion to the whole set up.

It was interesting to have a better second impression of a place, and its elevated quality now lent a lot of legitimacy to the sugar dating scheme. I found myself feeling intrigued again with a fresh surge of desire.

I walked around, inspecting each room. Zaneta's room was vibrant and inviting. I took in her suitcase, bursting with colourful dresses, trappings and costumes, stickered papers strewn on the table, drawn all over in bold markers—stars, sunshine, flowers, butterflies, a collection of uplifting words—POSITIVE, HOPE, INSPIRATION, LOVE, JOY, ABUNDANCE, GROWTH, GRATITUDE. Zaneta constantly worked on these themes— she was writing a dissertation on positive psychology for her extension school degree. My electric, happy-go-lucky princess. She never really grew up.

I wondered how she configured suicide assistance into her life's work. Or perhaps, she saw herself as bringing positivity into Covert's last years, and that made everything worth it in the end?

Covert's room looked less menacing under broad daylight. He made up the bed, the white sheet pulled tightly underneath the mattress, fluffy light gray cover spread on top. Unlike Zaneta's room, there were barely any trinkets, or any personal identifiers that gave me any clue on Covert's personality. There was his suitcase, black and practical. I opened the wardrobe and discovered a few striped shirts, a few white shirts, a few Bermudas, a couple of black pants. I saw a lined notebook opened to a page with faint, cursive handwritings neatly packed together. I did not try to read it.

There was a large jacuzzi with a bubble machine and pressure jets in Covert's bathroom, next to floor-to-ceiling glass windows overlooking the ocean. The shared bathroom in the living room was not nearly as grand, but there were patterned marble floors and gold-plated faucets and double shower heads. The toilet was placed inside a separate cubicle and its seat automatically heated up.

The whole place must be around 200 square metres, including the wraparound balcony. I took out my phone and did a quick google search of penthouse prices in this area. This place might very well cost between 1.5 to over two million USD—even if Zaneta and I were just to inherit this place and split it among us, we would have more than enough. She was not joking with her proposition.

I sat on the edge of Covert's bed for a while, digesting everything. I closed my eyes and imagined him on top of me, his toothbrush moustache scratching on my cheeks. I opened them again. *Everybody has a price.* Zaneta told me this.

Something caught the corner of my eye, a thin cord hanging from the ceiling. I looked up. There was a trap door, painted in the same white colour on the ceiling, with a very faint outline— almost as if it was not there. That was interesting. I never knew any penthouse with an attic before.

I rose from the bed and walked over to the spot right underneath the trap door, eyes still fixed to the ceiling. I reached up and pulled down the cord, but nothing happened. I squinted and saw that there was a latch on one side of the door, and it was secured with a tiny golden padlock. This door was locked.

'What are you doing?'

I looked behind my shoulders, Covert was standing just before the open door, forming a long shadow towards the bed. I wondered why I did not hear his footsteps.

'I just wanted to see what's up there.'

'You can't,' he said. 'The attic is off limits for you.'

'Why? What's up there?'

He shrugged. 'Just old belongings. Marge's. Things like her favourite clothes, diaries, letters between us . . . I carry them with me every time I travel and store them wherever I stay . . .'

'Why would you keep them a secret?'

'No, not a secret. I just don't . . . like people rummaging through her stuff, and potentially messing with them. I preserve everything exactly as they were when she passed. I don't . . . expect you to get it.'

I did not say anything. It was a little bit awkward, and I felt almost like a thief caught red-handed, even though I did nothing wrong.

'There, there Cassie, my curious cat. Stop getting yourself into trouble,' Zaneta chirruped into the room. She wrapped her arms around my shoulders and kissed me on the cheek. 'You heard what he said. Don't go around trying to break into the attic.'

She turned to Covert and blossomed with a smile. 'I know what I want for lunch. Mexican food. I need to get me some tacos now. And then, it's *my* turn to get a new bikini. I saw something I really liked the other day, at a boutique store. It is red with ribbons criss crossing all over the back. What do you think dear?'

'Uh-huh,' Covert beamed widely, and for the first time since I arrived in Florida, I felt a tinge of compassion for him. That look there he had for Zaneta, must be the same look I had been wearing for four years now.

My affair with Zaneta had not been following a straight trajectory. She eased me into her life and her lifestyle, bit by bit. In the beginning, she invited me to a lot of queer and sex positive parties in Boston—a network of misfits and trailblazers I would not have had access to otherwise.

I remembered seeing the drag queens perform a karaoke and burlesque showdown in a secret basement night club *The Machine*, nestled underneath one of the unassuming brownstone buildings at Beacon Hill. Their sequined tops sparkled under the disco lights; their tanned, muscled legs rippled as they opened and swung them around 180 degrees. They looked fantastic and magnificent—but neither was their beauty feminine nor masculine, it was exotic and otherworldly—the kind of beauty I had never seen in my life before.

Zaneta kept refilling my cup with gin and soda water, she preferred me being a little tipsy. In her own words, I was too 'self-conscious' otherwise.

We cheered and laughed as each of the magnificent drag queens performed their routines one by one, flashes of sparkled

sequined dresses, titanium blonde hair cascading and waving in a
blur of dreamlike motion, reflecting the colourful blinking disco
lights that rotated above our heads. 'Zaneta,' I turned to look at
her, my eyes wide. 'They were . . . something else.'

After the performance, the tallest of the ladyboys came to
our side, and gave Zaneta a big kiss on the cheek. 'Darling!' she
exclaimed. 'What a wonderful surprise! What brought you here on
a weekday night? And . . . who is this sweet little darling over here?
What's your name ma' dearest?'

'Cassie,' I smiled shyly.

'So, how did you find our performances darling?'

'Love it, absolutely mesmerizing. The best burlesque show
I have seen in my life.'

'Ahhh! You are too much, too much! How many burlesque
shows have you seen in your life?'

'Only . . . only this one' I said sheepishly.

'Pfft,' she pulled out a stick of cigarette, lit it and took a long
drag. 'Then I don't trust your standards darling,' she laughed
heartily. 'I'm Kate.' She extended her long-fingered hand. 'Pleasure
to meet.'

I knew where Zaneta acquired her sass from, if she had been
hanging out with this crowd.

The night continued to be dreamlike. Kate invited us back to
her place, with a bunch of other drag queens. There were a few
men too in the crowd—muscled, statuesque types who looked
too handsome to be straight.

We hung out on the rooftop, under the moonlight. A wrath
of orange light bulbs hung low above our heads, glinting like the
stars. A big fat joint was being passed around, we each took turns
to inhale, in a magical ceremony of sisterhood. I started seeing
shadows, dancing on the cement rooftop floors. There was a
rabbit, a girl, and a wizard wearing a tall hat.

The drag queens laughed melodiously, trading stories of men leering and paying them money to see more. They were popular, these ladyboys. Men from all ages and walks of life came to see them perform, bought them giant bouquets of flowers, invited them back to their places, and offered them more money.

'Are you ladies okay with it?' I asked at one point. 'I mean . . . being propositioned for sex.'

'Pfft, what nonsense!' one of the ladyboys with curly red hair by the name Margaret waved her hand dismissively. 'We girls are not obliged to make love to anyone we don't want to. Remember that. No amount of money or diamonds or flowers in the world can buy our love. Remember that. But of course, we are obliged to take the money when it comes *our way*!'

Zaneta started singing. Her voice chimed like jingle bells, as always, clear and precious.

Oh, happy day
Happy day we have here today
Where the fairies live joyful and free
Among a moonlit bed of roses, smelling fragrant
Like sweet, sweet love
That you and I, you and I embrace tonight

I wondered whether she wrote this song herself. One of the muscular guys came to sit on her lap and kissed her on the lips. Well, I guess not all of them were gay after all.

I watched them kiss passionately and I wished then that I could, went over to her lap and did the same.

Chapter Four

A Welcome Dinner

What does it take to educate a girl? How many years of schooling must she go through before she is fit to take on the world? What does it take to educate her on the Laws of Love? Who should be loved and how much to love and why and how?

At the age of eight, my parents sent me to a rigorous international school at the border of Tangerang town. It was decided that a formal education was appropriate to stop me from spending all my free time lying on the sofa reading romantic novels and Japanese comic books non-stop. It was September when I first enrolled in the school. Monsoon wind blew across dancing daffodils on grassy plains. Crickets chirped happily when the sun went down, and the weather grew comfortably cooler despite the perpetual sunny days.

The international school was a place where upper-middle-class Indonesian–Chinese families sent their children to get a better education in Java. It was run by a group of Javanese who had had Christian and Catholic education and therefore had adopted the protestant work ethics. It was better than the local neighbourhood school I would otherwise have attended.

I remembered memories from that school quite fondly. I remembered how teachers held mandatory chapel masses in the morning, in addition to the once-weekly mandatory school

ceremony under the scorching sun. I remembered how I read
my way to the canteen and to classes, past the popular boys who
played basketball with youthful dexterity. I remembered scoring
one hundred per cent for every examination, while ignoring the
teacher's admonition, and their frequent words of wisdom on
Godly virtues. I preferred to read instead. More than anything
I remembered 'the mean girls'. There were many, and they
conspired against me—the isolated girl, the arrogant smart kid
who built a fortress of books.

The mean girls consisted of four to five 'popular' girls
who navigated their way deftly among different social circles
in the class. These girls were neither overly intelligent nor
desperately half-witted. They were generally blessed with good
looks and their forté was the art of getting and granting favours
between themselves, based on the merits of social connection
and behaviour that were deemed 'acceptable' and 'agreeable'.
Gossiping and passing laudatory remarks to each other were
some obvious meritocratic behaviour. Reading books and
ignoring social conventions were not.

The mean girls in this school did not strike you openly, on
your way to classes. They did not slam your books to your face or
trapped you in your locker like the mean kids in American popular
TV shows often did. No, the mean girls would coyly gossip about
you in the bathroom, behind your back, and in-between lessons.
They would be humming gently and persistently, dropping dead
quiet once you showed up in their vicinity. Before the talks grew
quiet, they would take extra precaution that you heard your name
mentioned. 'Cassandra was—' and silence, awkward sly smiles
passed around. The discomfort was palpable. I had no other
choice but to look down with shame and rage I could not pinpoint
to anything. I knew they were calling me ugly and many other
names behind my back. I could not retaliate against anything
I had no proof of. Telling the teachers was futile, for the teachers

hated me for ignoring them, and doing so would bequeath me a reputation as a tattletale, thus making me prone to even more gossiping and mean side glances.

The mean girls in school looked at you with glassy eyes, filmy from their coloured contact lenses. I wondered why on earth did their parents allow them to wear contact lenses at such a young age. They knew the worth of such a feat. Coloured, trendy lenses fitting for celebrities and those who were 'in-the-know'. Not me, the bookworm with my big squarish glasses and fringes bunched into a fountain ponytail. One day I went up to the front of the History class to recite the Declaration of Independence. The mean girls were sniggering, gasping for air in between their cupped whispers to each other. Their glass eyes blinked in hilarity. When I stepped back to my bench, I realized that I had forgotten to zip my pants and they had been pointing at my white, oversized underwear all along. My neck, my cheeks, and my ears all grew red with shame. I stared at one of the leaders of the gang—Hannah, a stout girl with long brown hair and a mole on her face. 'Stop laughing or I would poke your eyeballs and squeeze those fake contacts out,' I hissed in a deep vibrating voice.

Hannah, taken aback by my violent threat, looked at her minions for support, but they too, fell silent at the prospect of having their glass eyes squeezed out.

'Cassie,' the class teacher who ignored their whispers and muffled laughter but suddenly became alert of my last sentence, called out my name. 'Go to the back of the class and remain there. Later after class see me in the office.'

The class teacher, Ms Chandra, was a middle-aged spinster who devoted her time to God and to work, in that order. She walked around with 'a perpetually deeply-aching heart' from years of 'witnessing our mischief and disrespect towards God.' She mumbled and complained and prayed, three to four times a day discounting nighttime when she returned to her childless homestead. I imagined her knitting and praying and crossing red marks on our spelling homework. Ms Chandra had wavy black hair and squinty eyes like a hamster. I only saw her in her green teacher uniform blazer, which hung too short over her hips, making her pudgier than she actually was.

In her air-conditioned office room that smelled of dried mothballs, Ms Chandra made me sit in front of her. She then drew up a bible and started to pray—'Dear God, bless this child for she does not know what she has done. Bless this child for she is bright, yet ignorant and young and she does not know that your power is always with us. Bless this child because she has committed wrongful actions and spoken wrongful words despite her knowledge in Your name. Bless this child and forgive her sins for she does not know that she has sinned . . .'

And on and on and on. Listening to her prayers was punishment in itself. I thought it was unfair. I was speaking up against injustice and I was punished as a result. She would not attack the mean girls for their network of connection reached far and complex to their parents' active involvement in the Parents—Teacher Association, a group responsible to raise funds for numerous school buildings and events. My father was often too drunk and my mother was too busy with her miserable life to participate in such extracurricular activities. Punishing me was the safer choice.

Looking back to this episode in my childhood, perhaps it was true that my ungodliness was the cause of my sufferings in subsequent years. My refusal to listen to the words of my teachers, the words of Jesus, and so on and so forth, precipitated in my downfall, my erroneous scandal with Zaneta.

Speaking of purity and God, these were the common themes that were rehashed over and over again by numerous respectable members of my school. Some of them went to the extent of delivering 'special speeches' every Friday or so, on the same messages around love, peace, sacrifice, and chastity. Madame Maria, the headmistress, took it into her hands to educate the girls on the value of their purity. One day she assembled all the girls after daily chapel and started to speak about—to everybody's surprise—boys.

'I have assembled all of you here today because most of you have reached puberty,' She began. Her tortoise-shell glasses perched dangerously on her flat nose. Her hair curly and dishevelled on her green teacher blazer's collar. 'You all are good, benevolent, sweet, little girls of God. You must maintain your purity for the man of your dreams. I know many of you have started to date the boys, talk with each other, and all that nonsense.' She breathed hard, her disapproval apparent.

'However, you are still very young. Just like a herd of cows that are going to be sacrificed to God, so are your bodies still pure and youthful and fitting to be sacrificed to Him. You must maintain this purity. Don't mar it with the boys. They don't deserve your purity. Your bodies are your temples, and you must take care of them so that when the time comes you would enter the holy matrimony with God and your future husband under His good graces and full approval. If, like a herd of cows sacrificed for God, you have tarnished your body and your reputation, then when you enter holy matrimony, it would not be holy and it would not be blessed anymore by Him. Remember my good girls, remember how important it is to keep your chastity.'

I listened to all this nonsense and raised my hand 'Where are the boys, Madame? Are we the only cows in this story?'

She told me to go see her separately after the talk.

Hence my reputation as the 'smarty pants who speaks up against the teachers'.

It was what I did best—questioning loopholes, looking for a flaw in puritan and double-standard instructions. Due to my good grades, there were high hopes looming above my head, whether I liked it or not, and despite my occasional clash with the authority, I never once skipped submitting a homework or failed to score near to perfect and perfect grades. I attributed my intelligence to my love for literature. I read voraciously—books, magazines, newspapers, food labels, anything that my hands could touch, and my eyes could read, I would read.

In the love department however, I was not as fortunate. His good graces that raised my grades did not prepare me well to win the boy who stole my heart. I spent full eight years of my existence, from the age of eight to the age of sixteen, pining after a handsome basketball player who happened to sit next to me in the school bus and quarrelled with me on everything under the sun, back and forth the daily journey of thirty-two kilometres from our suburban homes to the school at the other end of town. He moved on to junior high school and started acquiring his basketball player credentials among other older students, and subsequently, a pretty girlfriend to boot. I was crushed, yet it did not stop me from loving him from afar. I timed my toilet breaks to coincide with his basketball practices. I stole glances at his back on the basketball court during meal breaks.

Many years later, after my time in the United States ended, I would reconnect again with my first love, and we would go out for a cup of coffee at my initiation.

Sadly by then, the disappearance of Zaneta from my life left such a huge hole in my heart that it became numb to any romantic sensation for a good while. I could not feel a thing for the boy besides gratitude for meeting me. It seemed to me that this old, secret passion burning like relentless embers lighting the crevices of my heart had been extinguished completely, sucked into oblivion inside the black hole of loss and grief. A Zaneta-shaped hole in the universe, bigger than an old-crush-shaped hole in the universe. With the departure of Zaneta, along came the departure of Feelings with capital F.

We just had returned from our lunch at Taco Bell and some more bikini shopping at the mall. Covert ushered us back into the penthouse and Zaneta proceeded to throw herself on the sofa in the living room, twirling her platinum curls absent-mindedly. 'I am thinking you need to move to a bigger place, Covert.'

'What's wrong with my place now?'

'It's just . . . too old. Too musty. Too small. How are we ever going to throw a party here?'

Covert reached out to the shelf and poured himself a sip of whiskey, dropping clinking ice cubes into the glass. He smiled at her. 'Aren't we having a party . . . right now?'

'Pffttt, us?' Zaneta tilted her head and laughed. 'What about Bonnie?'

'What about her?' Covert was clearly in a good mood. When Zaneta chose to place her attention on anyone, she had that uplifting and intoxicating effect. 'I think we should have a nice dinner at the country club tonight. You, me, Cassie, Bonnie. It'll be Cassie's welcome dinner. Let's have a fancy feast!'

I went to the hanging mirror at the far end of the living room and checked on my hair, dishevelled in all sorts of wrong ways from the windy beach. 'What are we going to eat?' I felt like I should be saying something sweet or funny, in return for his generous gesture, but nothing came to mind.

'Lobster,' Zaneta came behind me and wrapped her hands around my waist, staring squarely into the mirror. 'Scallops. Fish. Premium greens. Beef. Roast duck. It could be a buffet if you want it.' She smelled like vanilla and cinnamon. 'Look at this face,' her long index finger and thumb pinched at my chin. 'Look at how adorable you are.'

'Where is this place? Should we dress up?'

'Sure sweetie, sure we do.'

Zaneta grabbed my wrist, pranced into her room and pulled out a suitcase. It was overflowing with puffy fabric, numerous rough organza dresses in garish colours—pink and yellow and blue and green. There were white gauzy ruffles everywhere, stitched-on pearls in pastel colours, silver and golden beads. 'Come, check out my Disney princess dresses. What colour would you like?'

'Are you seriously going to wear *this*? To a dinner?' I laughed at her.

'Yes, why not? I'd love to make a scene,' she grinned.

I picked the green one, it had a silk bodice and a zipper at the back. A huge white rose perched on top of the left shoulder. 'Oh man, check this out,' I giggled.

We closed the bedroom door on Covert and started changing. I had to squeeze myself into the silk green bodice and sucked my breath to zip up. The ruffles gave me itches and it made excessive noises every time I moved.

'Hold on, there is a lace cap that goes with that,' Zaneta placed a small green cap on top of my head, it had a delicate lace veil falling gently to cover my face. I looked like I was about to attend a tea with the Queen.

She herself changed into a puffy dress that looked like mine, only glittery purple in colour. She painted her lips in dark red and her lids in shadows of gold. Our costumes described might sound cheap and over the top, but only on Zaneta, fabrics shone with an elevated fairytale glow. I wished that just by being around her, some of her magic would rub off on me.

Bonnie knocked on our apartment door close to 7 p.m. That was the first time I saw her. She had dark red hair, the colour of rust, pale milky skin and large soft eyes. She was wearing a red puffy dress that could have come from Zaneta's collection as well. 'Welcome my lady,' Zaneta curtsied at her. Bonnie did not even have to try, she belonged in Disneyland.

'Where is Rex?' asked Zaneta.

'It's his nap time. Drew got him under control,' Bonnie flashed a smile. 'And you must be Cassie?'

'Yes,' I gave a small smile. 'I've heard tons about you.' *And your breastmilk.*

Covert came out of his bedroom, clad in a suit. He had waxed his moustache and twirled the ends into pointy shapes. I did not know anyone who actually did that. 'Ah Bonnie, Bonnie. I'm so glad you could join us at such a short notice.'

He opened his arms and gave her two pecks on the cheeks, squeezed her breasts. Bonnie looked delighted. 'These babies are almost ready for you . . . They are going to get heavy real soon . . .'

I winced. I wondered how much she got paid, though her smile seemed genuine, and her eyes shone when she looked at him. I supposed love came in many shapes and forms.

Ali came to pick us up with his limousine. He did not seem to recognize me when he ushered all of us into the car. I figured he would not be able to keep track of every single girl that Covert had invited over for the weekends.

Our ballooning skirts rubbed against each other in the backseat of the limousine. I had to squeeze myself close to the windowpane to make room for everyone. The limousine sped past the beach, onto the roads with flat buildings and palm trees.

Bonnie and Zaneta giggled with Covert the whole journey, like proper lovers in love. They were teasing and touching each other's hair, poking here and there, shrieking and laughing. I wondered whether they had taken any drugs without telling me. I felt left out of an important joke.

We pulled over at the courtyard in front of a white terracotta building with red-brick shingled roofs. There was a circular marble fountain in the middle of the courtyard. Sleek limousines and sports cars stopped one after another, expelling older white men and women wearing furs, pearls, and bow ties and suits.

Inside the country club, high-ceilinged rooms connected with one another through a series of stuccoed white and golden pillars. The walls were painted deep cerulean blue. Waiters and waitresses glided in and out of rooms carrying silver domed trays. A lady in a silk dress tinkered with graceful tunes on a piano in the corner.

Our group attracted some questioning eyes, which delighted Zaneta. She sashayed her way into the middle of the establishment, where a waiter directed us to a circular table clothed in white. An older woman with blonde curls seated next to us eyed Zaneta from head to toe and whispered to her husband, who looked almost like Covert. The woman could barely hide her disgust when Covert appeared behind Zaneta. I thought she might almost throw up on the table. Zaneta winked at her.

We all took a seat. Bonnie tossed her head back and laughed at everything Covert had to say. 'Look at this wiener—eh. It has the weirdest shape. I swear it looks like my distant uncle's . . .' Bonnie shrieked hysterically . . . and, 'Zaneta dear, I dare you . . . to inquire with the gentleman of a waiter right there . . . if he knows whether patrons of this country club . . . *have sex in the bathroom.*'

At that point in the evening, I had decided that Bonnie must be sincerely in love with the old man. She could not have possibly faked all those high-pitched laughters, and the constant hair-tossing, and eyelash batting. I wondered about Covert's 'beautiful cock' and pictured them together on the bed, him grunting and sweating red like a boiled crab, his lips curled behind his toothbrush moustache. Bonnie with her milky white curves, her breasts heaving in tandem with his thrusts, head lolling back in ecstasy.

Zaneta touched my elbow. 'Hey sweetie, would you come with me for a sec? Let's take pictures on the grass, by the sunset, in our dresses.'

I followed her outside to a robust lawn that sprawled into a distant golf course. The sun was a liquid golden yolk in the horizon, spilling red bursts all over the clouds. There were slivers of lakes like sparkling tiny diamonds to the northeast and to the west. Zaneta's purple dress shimmered like a vision. She looked simultaneously attuned and out of place with her surroundings. The platinum blonde in stark contrast with the deep blue-orange sky.

We took turns taking pictures. I looked at mine and cringed. My skin was pasty, my smile wan. The balloon green dress looked ridiculous instead of ethereal.

'Quit it,' Zaneta said. 'Quit insulting yourself. You know that your words shape your reality.'

We strolled on the freshly cut grass, hand in hand, watching the sun set behind a stack of clouds and the sky turned colour into velvet black. The stars started to twinkle. 'Are you enjoying yourself, love?'

'I do now,' I squeezed her hand back. 'It's quite interesting. I think Bonnie really likes him.'

Zaneta took a deep breath. 'Tell me about it. If only she could take over, she'd be perfect. However, she has a husband and a baby . . . One sec—it's Blake on the phone . . .'

She let go of my hand to take out her cell phone from her purse. 'Hey babe, what's up?' She walked further down the field of grass and mumbled into the phone. 'Yes, sure. Mmhmm. Yes. I'm sorry to hear that babe. I hope things will get better . . .'

I found myself staring into space, basking in the warm and windy night. I considered calling someone too, but I could not decide who—my mom, my dad, my sister? They were all about twelve hours apart. Perhaps my roommate Beverly, whom I knew from the theater group. We attended dance classes together, went to parties on campus and copied each other's homework, but that was about it. What could I possibly tell her? *Hey, I'm in Florida, doing a recce on an after-graduation sugardating-suicide gig. How's your spring break going?*

Zaneta came back to me, her brows frowned in a way that I did not expect. 'Is anything the matter?'

'Blake worries me,' she said in a low voice. 'He's been having his bouts of depression again, and it's getting worse and worse. It's his dissertation. He is stuck. And he thinks I might leave him for Covert, but he also can't meet the rent, and I make very good money here.'

'I'm sorry to hear.' My voice fell flat. I was not sure whether there was any easy solution to this situation.

'Wouldn't it be nice . . . when all of this is over, eh?' She smiled. 'Imagine the possibilities. We could be in Barcelona now, travelling with all the money we could possibly need.'

'It does sound nice.' I thought to myself where I would go, and with whom. I would follow Zaneta to the end of the world, though I might stick out like a sore thumb, an awkward third wheel.

We turned and walked back to the country club. The clock showed seven o'clock, we had been gone for close to forty-five minutes. The dishes had been served on the table. Covert was munching on a piece of ribeye steak and Bonnie nibbled on a grilled sea bass.

'There you are! The ladies of the hour! Where did you two disappear to?' Covert chuckled with his mouth full.

Zaneta squeezed his shoulder and gave him a peck on the cheek. 'I'm sorry sweetheart. We got lost wandering around watching the sunset.'

'Cassie! This is your welcome dinner dear. You gotta look a little bit more excited!' Covert offered one hand to me, but I pretended not to take notice.

I sat down and started on the pasta and chicken. I was wondering whether this spring break was a probation period for me and whether I would pass the test. I knew I had not been giving the best of impressions.

I stayed quiet and chewed things that tasted like rubber, washed down with gulps of acidic champagne. Covert constantly threw one lame joke after another, Bonnie was laughing somewhere

close. Zaneta chimed in at intervals. Everything started to buzz
into a blur at my periphery. It all didn't quite make sense to me,
all of it. I was not sure why we were here in the first place, and
whether any of us was actually having fun.

I set down my cutleries, they clattered on my empty plate with
a clang louder than I had expected. Bonnie stopped her laughter
midway. Covert and Zaneta looked up from their plates.

'Covert,' I heard my voice loud and clear, reaching across the
table. 'Why would you want to kill yourself?'

Everything stood still for a second. Bonnie blinked in confusion.
Zaneta threw me a sharp glance, which I steadfastly ignored.

'I would like to know the story now, please, if you don't mind.'

Covert was not smiling, he looked flustered at the sudden
attack. He wiped his mouth with a napkin and smacked his lips
several times.

'Sweetheart . . . You don't have to . . .' Zaneta started, but he
put his hand up in the air.

'That's fine dear, that's fine. It's fair for her to know.' He
looked at me. 'Truth is . . . I do it for love, Cassie . . . what else
could it be, eh?'

'It was the love of my life . . . my wife Margie. She had multiple
sclerosis and she passed away a while back . . . Two years ago . . .
Just before I met Zaneta. Margie told me . . . she told me to follow
her into the afterlife. So I'm keeping to my promise.'

I stared at him. I would not know how it would be like to love
someone so much that your life became pointless without.

'I love my wife, I really do, with all my heart. I loved her then,
I love her now. There has not been a single day gone by without
me thinking of her, every single morning. We were together for
sixty solid years. She was my first love, my high school sweetheart,
my college sweetheart. She was my business partner. I don't see
any other life worth living without her in it.'

Bonnie wrapped her arms around his shoulders and buried
her nose into his neck.

'How . . .' I stammered, 'How did she pass away?'

'Naturally, on her bed,' Zaneta chipped in quickly. 'She was put on a breathing machine in her final year—all her major internal and external muscles had degenerated. She passed away in her sleep. The day before her passing, she told Covert to join her eventually.'

Covert said, 'I told her—"I'm gonna give myself three years to think it through. I'm gonna live my life until then." I started with sugar babies right after she left me. But no one else ever compares. No one.'

'It's up to you Cassie,' He sighed, reaching out for the open bottle of wine on the table and poured himself a glass. 'Nobody forced you to be here, wasn't it? You came willingly. What did you expect?'

'What do you want from me?'

Covert sipped his wine. 'Companionship. Companionship now and in the last year of my timeline. Zaneta told me about your work permit situation. I think this is going to be a good arrangement for all of us.'

I felt my ears ringing and my cheeks growing hot with an intense emotion I could not describe. Not in my wildest imagination would I expect such a story. I was expecting Covert to tell me that he was sick with terminal illness.

Another silence descended upon our table. Now I understood what it was that had been bothering me the whole time—the gravity of grief. It was so palpable now I could almost touch it.

'I don't think . . .' I started finally, breaking the precarious silence. 'I don't think it is legal . . . anywhere . . . To kill yourself if you weren't . . . if you weren't sick. I don't think you could do it Covert.'

To my horror Covert started to break down crying, first whimpering in little gulps and finally choking tearful big sobs. His whole face crumpled into a pained expression. He trembled like a leaf in Bonnie's arms.

The few people in the restaurant looked up. The lady next to our table whispered even more furiously to her husband. A waiter came over and silently cleared our dishes, then placed the bill on the table without being asked.

'There, there, there. That's enough for now,' Zaneta decided sternly. She helped Covert to get up and glared at me. 'Next time Cassie, think before you speak, I beg of you. There is no point hurting him like that.'

Chapter Five

Our Happily Ever After

There was a time when Covert was a sprightly young man, finishing a degree in biochemistry at Middlebury College. He was in love with a girl who studied film at Wesleyan, and so he would attend jam-packed classes from Mondays to Thursdays and by 2 p.m. on Thursday afternoons, would jump onto his dusty grey Buick to take the I-91 highway all the way down to Connecticut to visit his sweetheart. It was a four-hour drive south, sometimes five in bad traffic.

Covert put on soulful country songs on his cassette tape player most times, finding companionship in the saccharine twang of men just like him, pining for their Jenny and Charlene and Alyssa, Rosie and Genevieve and Desiree.

It was Margaret, the name of his sweetheart. They grew up in the same neighbourhood in Raleigh, North Carolina. They went to the same church, and their mothers' exchanged eggs, sugar and gossip in each other's kitchens.

Margaret was a bewitching red head, with jade green eyes and pearly, milky, skin. They knew each other for a very long time, yet never had a reason to say a word to each other.

She was painfully shy and quiet, yet whenever they passed each other in their high school corridors, Covert swore that she would let her gaze linger a little bit longer on his face, before she lowered her thick lashes down to the floor. Always, that slight, demure gesture sent him into wild speculations that kept him awake at night.

One night, almost feverish from the thought of Margaret's full, pouting lips when he spotted her at the cafeteria earlier, Covert jumped off his bed, driven by such an irrational gusto that clouded his sights and kept his ears ringing. He climbed out of his bedroom windows and slid down the water pipe, rolled onto the grass and ran to Margaret's house across the street. He knew exactly where her bedroom was, as he had spied on her often through her windows, whenever her curtains were drawn open.

He started climbing the water pipe on the walls of the house. Covert had always been a competent athlete, and so he hoisted himself effortlessly from footing to footing, further up the whitewashed brick walls. Finally he balanced himself on the protruding ledge of the second floor and knocked on Margie's windows. 'Margaret,' he knocked. 'Margaret!'

The lace curtain shifted, and then pulled to the side. Margaret stood there in her silvery nightgown. Her nipples stood erect and almost visible behind the thin lacy material. Her auburn flaming locks fell in cascade down to her back.

Margaret opened her windows without saying a word. She held his gaze, quiet and steady, and helped him step into the room. His breath hurried, he clasped his hands around her tiny waist.

'Margaret . . .' he sighed.

She raised her index finger to his lips. 'Sssshh . . .' and then. 'Call me Margie. Please.'

He buried his nose into her fragrant neck and breathed in deeply. His hands travelled to cup both of her budding breasts and squeezed hard, almost with rage. Margie whimpered. Covert felt his own erection bulge so tight against his zippered pants it was hurting him.

That night he claimed her over and over again in her pastel-coloured childhood room, with an insatiable fire that burnt deep within his core. That fire, he professed, would remain inextinguishable for years and years to come.

———————————

'I spent all of my weekends in college at her tiny dorm room in Wesleyan,' Covert recalled. 'I was obsessed. We were inseparable.'

We were seated back in Covert's penthouse apartment, still in our sparkly ruffled dresses. I thought this presented a hilarious scene, but his story felt too important to interrupt by a change of attire.

Covert and Margie had a smooth-sailing romance, one most people coveted as the ideal manifestation of true love—high school sweethearts, first love that lasted forever, passion that burnt bright and steady.

After Covert finished his degree, he got a clerical job in a pharmaceutical company in Boston. Margie joined him, taking freelance gigs at a local twenty-four-hour TV station. In her free time, she produced low-budget indie movies that circulated at little-known film festivals.

They rented a small room with a queen bed, in a three-bedroom apartment in North End. Covert went to work in the mornings, and Margie went to work in the evenings, so they rarely saw each other. On the weekends though, he made her breakfast in bed and took her to the museums, or theatrical shows, or wine tasting at local pubs.

He made decent money at the pharmaceutical company and was showing promises to climb the ranks in the company management. For a while life was good and steady. They made love often, they laughed often. He was saving for a destination wedding, perhaps a property, and a new upgrade of his old Buick.

When Covert decided to quit his promising career to start an export-import medical equipment business on his own, Margie hugged him tightly and told him that she was proud of him.

They moved to a smaller apartment in Jamaica Plains. The old floorboards were spotted with mildew and the windows were not closing properly so cold-biting air sneaked into the rooms in the winters. Margie had to take day shifts waiting tables at a gourmet restaurant downtown to make up for their rent, while Covert poured his savings into his new company.

'She supported me, all the way, through it all. Thick and thin, health and sickness. We almost never fought.'

This was a fascinating piece of information. I recalled my own volatile parents, screaming and yelling, hot angry tears, broken plates and upturned chairs. 'My parents said no couple is perfect,' I interrupted, unnecessarily.

Covert gave me a look. 'Sure. We fought for a fair bit, but never for too long. We did not have the heart to be angry at each other for very long.'

'We were obsessed, we could not live without each other, and we loved it that way. Now that I reflected, that was probably the main reason we did not have any children. There was never the right time . . . we enjoyed each other so much. Children would ruin our marital bliss. I certainly *did not* want to share her love and attention with anyone. Well if you could say so, perhaps our imperfection was that we loved each other *too much*. Too much. I would follow her to the ends of the earth. I would join her in the afterlife . . .'

'It certainly does sound a little bit codependent . . . if you want my opinion . . .' I chimed in, but quickly stopped myself as I sensed Zaneta's gaze burning holes at the back of my neck.

Covert and Margaret did not have to struggle for very long. Covert's intuition proved to be spot on and his business took off to great heights. He was soon catering to big hospitals in the countries, reputable pharmaceutical companies including his previous employer, bioengineering startups and healthcare factories. He had a business partner in China who supplied him with anything from gloves to fine surgical equipment to high-tech imaging devices at a fraction of the cost in the US.

'Remember this was in the late seventies, when the US started opening trade again with China, so I became the first player who snatched this golden window of opportunity. I was at the right time, at the right place, with the right idea. My previous job obviously helped with all the networking and connections.'

'How did you find your business partner in China?' I questioned, taking mental notes. Opportunities! Success! Escape from mind-numbing employment!

'Well by chance actually . . . Completely by chance. I met this bright young lad at a trade show, he was visiting from Shenzhen and he pitched me this idea. His family had been in the industry for a long time, but it was all domestic. It was a stroke of luck that I trusted him and we struck a fruitful partnership. It was a leap of faith for both sides of the party.'

A leap of faith. A stroke of luck. A golden window of opportunity. The right chance, the right timing, the right places, the right people . . . 'right' being the key operative word here. Was it not the case for everything else in life? Hard work and talent could only get you so far, most of the time you were feeling your way in the dark, blindly, believing that you were going somewhere. And only in the aftermath, and as an afterthought, you looked back and saw how things truly clicked together in your favor. 'Aha,' you would say, 'I was lucky. I seized the opportunity. I was ready.'

It fell onto my lap, I imagined myself saying this to an audience of skimpily clad, sculpted bodies at my private yacht party in the Bahamas, two years down the road. *I was ready to rise to the occasion. It was the right timing, the right place, the right opportunity, the right people . . .*

Covert's hand rested at the base of my lower back, and it jolted me out of my daydreaming. 'Well the rest is history,' he said. 'As you could see, here . . .' he waved at his penthouse. 'This old thing right here. And I have a few other upscale properties all over the country. The business is still in operation, fully profitable, and it has gone public. I have stocks, I have cash, I have gold, I have everything . . . But why would any of this matter without Margie by my side?'

His hand travelled up and down my back.

'You could . . . Perhaps pick a new hobby?' I offered. 'Take on a new challenge? Pick up a cause to fight in the world? Why . . . why would she ask you to die . . . If she had truly loved you? I would want my loved ones to continue living without me, to enjoy life to the fullest, to be happy and healthy as long as possible.'

Covert chuckled, and thankfully, withdrew his hand. 'Dear, dear, Cassie, dear. You truly have no idea what real love looks like, do you?'

How would I understand what love looked like? My parents? I remembered Father returning home, plonking himself on the sofa, calling out to my mother for a bucket of steaming hot water to soak his feet in. His breath smelled like alcohol, his eyes bloodshot and tired. I remembered father counting wads of cash and passing them to Mother with a grunt, father asking her what's cooking for dinner, father gathering his keys and leaving again in the middle of the night.

They neither laughed nor conversed at length, though I did not sense that she feared him in any way. Her disposition was more of a quiet resignation, as there was nothing more to be expected.

When the Ambonese came to meet Father in the living room, Mother would tell us to stay in our bedrooms and keep quiet. She did not like to talk to them herself, preferring to keep busy in the kitchen cleaning the countertops.

However, there was one time when I came back from my outdoor playtime with the neighbours and I saw five of them already seated in the living room, drinking hot tea and chewing fried bananas that our maid Siti prepared. Their teeth looked very white in contrast to their dark round faces.

One of them wore so many gold rings and bracelets on his fingers and wrist. He grinned at me, and I saw one gold tooth in the corner. I took him to be the leader of the gang. 'Look at you, little girl, how sweet you are . . .'

'This is my youngest daughter, bro,' my father reached out and tapped my head endearingly. I was surprised yet immensely delighted by this rare gesture.

'Such a lovely family you have here Boss, lovely family.'

'It would be very very unfortunate should anything happen to your family, Sir,' added another one. He was shorter, but bulkier, with thick, black, broom-like hair that fell to his shoulders. A huge white scar ran from the corner of his right eyes down to his lips.

Father looked significantly distressed today, and the whole room was heavy with tension. I figured Mother and my sister must be upstairs in the bedrooms, as always.

'If what you were telling me were right . . .'

'It's all confirmed Boss,' the gold-toothed person nodded seriously. 'The plan would be launched somewhere mid-May. All of us on the streets already knew about this, plans had been disseminated early this year. There was only one instruction—loot and make chaos so that the incumbent president should resign.'

'And *spare no Chinese*,' the broom-haired person hissed menacingly. 'Especially the wealthy ones.'

Father went white, little beads of sweat formed on his temple.

I did not understand any of this much back then. I knew that many people around me did not look like me—they had darker skin and bigger eyes. However everybody in school did look like me, with yellow skin and squinty eyes, and as I mostly interacted with people at school, it did not bother me too much.

'We are truly truly grateful for our friendship with our Chinese brothers so far, Boss, truly grateful,' Gold Tooth nodded. The whole gang murmured in agreement. 'You've basically fed us . . . Since my boy was this big.' He gestured his right hand close above the ground.

'Which is why we are telling you all these today,' Broom Hair chimed in. 'You all need to know beforehand. You all need to flee. Singapore perhaps. Hong Kong?'

The two of them seemed to be the only ones with the mental faculty to speak. Grim silence hung above our heads, somewhat interrupted with the persistent sound of teeth grinding and lips smacking from the rest of the gang chewing on banana fritters with deadpan faces.

Father stared blankly onto the table in front of him. He seemed to be at a loss for words. Finally after what felt like forever, the gold-toothed person stood up from his seat. He nodded at the rest, signaling them to follow along. 'It's about time we make our move, Boss,' he said. Father nodded, not meeting their eyes.

The gold-tooth rested one hand upon his shoulder. 'And if it doesn't trouble you much Boss . . . something to cover our gas fees for travelling all the way here today . . .'

'Huh?' Father looked almost like he was ambushed. His jaw dropped and for a second he looked like a very old man. He quickly collected himself. 'Oh, of course. Sure. Understood.' He reached into his pocket and pulled out a wad of cash, counted a handful of notes and handed them to the Gold Tooth.

Broom Hair cupped his hands in front of his chest and made an awkward *kowtow* gesture. 'Thank you very much Boss! Shalom and God bless!'

'Shalom!' The rest of the gang finally spoke in unison.

After they left, Father turned to look at me and spoke carefully, 'Let's not mention any of this to your mother or your sister . . . yet. Do you understand?' He ruffled my hair fondly 'Tell them we are going to go for a vacation to Singapore.'

I suppose that's what love looked like in our family.

* * *

We departed for Singapore right as the riot was erupting. On the television someone was telling the story of a big student commotion at the heart of the city, of a gunshot firing somewhere in the distance, of people screaming and dispersing and being carted off to hospital.

On our car ride to the airport, we pressed through thick throngs of masses crowding the street. I saw a car being thrown upside down, bursting in flames. Everything was moving in a water-like slow motion. My sister was crying. I stared wide-eyed outside the window, with a mixture of both fear and excitement. 'Something is happening,' I whispered to her.

Mother gripped the armrest of the car seat, her knuckles white, her face tense with anticipation. She turned to my sister and patted her head. 'Ssshh . . . there, there. Everything is going to be alright . . .' I had never seen her being so gentle with my sister before.

The airport was filled with people who looked like us, carrying suitcases and crying babies. Everyone seemed to be in a lot of rush. Father kept checking at his phone, beads of sweat forming on his temple.

'What are you doing? Stop looking at your phone,' Mother scolded.

'There are things I need to settle with the boys,' said Father.

We arrived in Singapore that night. A black sedan drove us to a hotel, where the four of us stayed in one big room. Mother told us not to turn on the TV. We stayed mostly inside and ordered food for a few days, when finally, Father, looking up from his cell phone, switched the TV on and tuned into an Indonesian channel.

There was a new President. There was a serious speech about the economy, autonomy and defense. The Declaration of Independence was evoked multiple times. I did not know what was going on exactly but it felt like something heavy and fearful, important and transformational was happening. It felt like there was a heavy lead at the pit of my stomach.

Father talked to Mother in muffled voices . . . 'Uncle so and so has passed . . . So has Aunty so and so . . . the whole family was . . . Blood all over the streets . . .' They both looked pale and sickly.

We stayed in Singapore for about a month, loitering aimlessly during the day in the shopping malls and cafes, in public parks and museums before going back to our cramped hotel room. Mother stopped her usual bouts of crying during this period, suddenly pulled herself together, appearing like she was guided by a newfound purpose. She made sure that we were clean and well-fed. She combed out our hair and sang nursery rhymes. The TV remained turned off the whole month except for that one-time Father switched it on during the election.

Father, on the other hand, was the one who seemed to be losing his mind, perpetually glued to his cell phone. He paced around the room constantly, stared outside the window absent-mindedly. He looked sickly worried still and refused to touch his food. 'What is going on with you?' Mother was visibly irritated. 'Are you going to worry yourself to death with the situation back home? Just wait until the storm is over and stop constantly worrying over things!'

One day, Mother was out taking a walk with my sister and Father was in the bathroom. I saw Father's phone vibrate, the green glow on the screen illuminated black letters, it said 'Cinta', which means 'love'. It rang and rang for a few minutes. Instinctively I threw a pillow over it, even though I was not sure why I did so. When Father came out of the bathroom, he looked at the pillow over the tabletop, removed it, took his phone. He looked at me, but he did not say anything.

We flew back to Jakarta a few days later. The words on the streets were that a good number of people, of our kind, had passed away—raped, looted, burnt. We drove past dead, empty buildings with smashed windows and charred walls, and corpses of cars covered in ashes and smoke.

A new era had begun.

Chapter Six

Faster, Baby, Faster

In my sophomore year, I attended a Harvard class on sex and desire. It was offered under the gender studies department, by a buxom professor from Jamaica who had thick curly hair sticking out of her head like wires. She told us about 'penis envy', the unconscious phenomenon present in women that leads them to desire for a penis.

The desire for owning a penis, manifests in girls turning to their fathers for fulfillment and blaming their mothers for being responsible for the lack thereof. It said so in my textbook that had a black-and-white print caricature of Sigmund Freud on its cover.

The penis envy leads to either a woman being overly inhibited or overly loud and masculine, and only when this desire for a penis is replaced by a desire for a child, a woman would finally feel truly integrated in her feminine self. She would feel the greatest joy when she would give birth to a child, and especially so if the child is a boy, for she would be redeeming her lack of penis by giving birth to a penis.

I digested and thought about this carefully. The Jamaican professor was drawing a big penis in chalk on the black board, complete with bushy undergrowth. It looked like a tree.

'Man, what a downer. I was so excited about this class,' whispered a kid seated next to me, wearing a backward baseball cap. 'I thought it was going to be about . . . *sex.*'

'Now, what do we think about this? Would you agree, or disagree? And why?' She finished shading her penis with a flourish.

A brunette raised her finger. 'I would think this "penis envy" concept is the clearest proof for male chauvinism that has permeated the annals of psychoanalysis since its inception.' She looked red and deeply offended. Her voice vibrated with emotion.

'And why would you say so?' The professor smiled encouragingly. I would assume that she liked where the brunette was going.

'Well, this is made on the premise that the penis is indeed superior genitalia, and that we, deficient women, could not help but desire to have it, just because it has more flesh to show. This is absolute nonsense to me. I could theoretically posit that men experience "vagina envy" for they know that the vagina is the source of life, and by default vaginas give birth to any penis that has ever existed on earth.'

To this end, all the female students in the room clapped with gusto. Someone even did a standing ovation. The baseball-capped-kid looked a little bit fearful.

I thought about this a little bit more and raised my hand.

'Yes, girl at the back?' The professor flashed her big white teeth.

'I think perhaps Freud might have been just . . . describing the human condition.'

'Alright,' she nodded. 'What do you mean by that?'

'There is a certain truth to her statement,' I looked at the brunette carefully. 'Sure it can be argued as a form of male chauvinism, but judging that our society has been under patriarchy for a long time . . . isn't it logical for a woman to envy being born a man? And isn't it logical that being able to procreate solidifies her position in the society and especially so if she gives birth to a man? I would rather argue that the subconscious penis envy talk was a purported psychoanalytical hypothesis that simply describes the state of our society.'

The professor looked pleased with herself. The rest of the females in the room clapped again, including the brunette.

The class lasted another half an hour more, but I was barely listening anymore. I was happy to be able to engage meaningfully in an impractical discussion about penis that should score me a few brownie points. My strategy for a minimum of A minus was to chip in at least one memorable comment at every class. 'No matter how stupid you may sound, just keep going,' Becky, my South Korean roommate, advised me sincerely last year. 'Just keep the hell going.'

That was one of the most valuable lessons I had gotten out of Harvard.

I always remembered the gold, the opulence, the glittering excesses. There were always colonnaded walkways and balustrades in white, excellent marbles, tinged with gold streaks, topped with intricate friezes. Plush, red velvet carpet into which my heels sunk smoothly. Extravagant crystal chandeliers and painted ceilings, usually depicting winged angels on the backdrop of silver clouds and cerulean skies.

It was almost comical, all these grand stylised gestures that mimicked classical Greek or Roman architecture—but with a twist of Chinese flavour—usually in the form of gigantic granite lions and dragons guarding every entrance, and as always—big gold mandarin letters protruding across glass walls, streams of water pouring behind it. The letters always said the most elaborate, ridiculous names, saturated with meanings associated with prosperity, divinity or longevity—Seven Skies Advancing Life Casino Royale, The Eight Gods Empire Wonderland Casino, Long Live Emperor and Empress on The Heavenly Realm Casino.

I had frequented many such establishments across East Asia and Southeast Asia—Macau and Singapore, Taipei and Shanghai, Manila and Genting—they all had almost the same characteristics, probably built by the same handful of developers. They reflected the new wealth of the Chinese diaspora, a world replete with the accumulation and display of luxurious goods. Men walked around with pomaded hair, leather loafers and tailored flamboyant suits, they liked to pin flowers on top of their pockets and smoked Cuban cigars wrapped in gold papers. The ladies looked almost uniformly pale and skinny, with heavy make-up and fake eyelashes, well-coiffed hair, off-shoulder silky dresses. They carried similar-looking bags, wore stiletto heels studded in precious stones. Only a few European brands were acceptable in this environment—the likes of Gucci, Hermès, Louboutin—each piece at the price tag of tens of thousands of dollars.

Mostly I associated them with Father, these spaces were his natural habitat. When he walked through the glass doors and stepped onto the velvet red carpet, his eyes lit up with joy and belonging. He rubbed his hands with excitement, he greeted everyone, called everyone 'bro', exchanged news on business affairs and the latest development of their family members.

He would grab a glass of red wine from the passing waiter and told me to greet everyone 'Uncle' or 'Aunty'. They usually passed a few sentences discussing my appearance, without expecting me to say anything in return. 'She has grown taller,' 'She seems to have put on some weight, better be careful', 'Oh, how she looks just like your wife now!'

Mother did not like to come down with us, preferring to stay in the hotel room, watching TV and ordering dinner. I knew that she would be wrapped in a bathrobe all day long, taking long hot baths in the jacuzzi and blasting cheesy eighties music at maximum volume.

Since turning seventeen, before moving to the United States, I never missed an opportunity to go in with Father, usually on weekend trips and school breaks. I liked dressing up in Mother's gown, wearing heels that were slightly too big for my feet, and putting on loud red lipstick.

I felt instantaneously more mature, more elegant, more powerful. I told myself that since Mother was often absent, Father depended on me to take the escorting role, to flaunt branded shoes and bags and jewellery that he bought for her. Most of the ladies were there as plus ones, rarely would they gamble themselves in the card rooms.

My sister refused to go on any of these trips. While I grew up perpetually curious to get into my father's world, my sister had decided early on that she needed to rise above all the sins of the flesh that had become the source of material sufferings and Mother's tears. She took up Buddhism very seriously, chanting mantras every morning and night and went to join *Puja* ceremonies every Sunday. The rest of her free time outside of school was spent on watching and listening to Dharma podcasts and videos. My sister grew into an old woman much earlier than her time.

Inside the casino, after making one round greeting and chatting with everyone, Father would tell me to indulge in the buffet spread, while he proceeded to one of the card rooms with a group of men his age.

The buffet spread was equally extravagant and excessive: rows of white clothed long tables bearing premium seafood and meat and cheese—lobsters, crabs, white fluffy fish, shark fin soup, caviar, roast duck, pork and chicken dumplings. On the other side there were sushi and avocados, and a smaller spread of Western dishes, pastas and bread. Bowls of fresh tropical fruits and warm soup dessert beckoned at me. Somehow though, I found it hard to work up an appetite, it felt ungainly to feast to my heart's content wearing such a glamorous outfit, for fear of spoiling my red lipstick. I noticed most of the ladies only picked at their plates, holding long white cigarettes with their manicured fingers, staring into the distance.

There was always a grand piano, next to a small water fountain or a crackling fireplace, or both. There was always a man in a suit playing romantic Chinese songs on the piano, and a slender young songstress in a traditional body—hugging *qibao* singing into the microphone. I sat at the table next to the piano, swaying gently to the tune, picking at orange fish roe from my sushi plate.

After eating, there was nothing much to do really. I would grow bored at this point. I would wander around the carpeted hallways, looking at people playing games on the blinking slot machines. Father never gave me any coin to play, so I looked at the machines patiently and made a bet with myself—if this lady here struck three strawberries in a row, Father would come and get me. If she missed, I would walk another round and grab something else from the buffet.

He was somewhere inside one of the card rooms, either playing blackjack or baccarat, his favourite games. Sometimes he played poker too. He never taught me any of these games, so they remained a mystery, dealt behind heavy oak-panelled doors along the VIP corridor. Sometimes one of these doors would swing open and a man stepped outside to smoke or to use the restroom. I caught a glimpse of dark-green walls and more red velvet carpet, round colourful tables huddled with men shouting expletives in various Chinese dialects. Card dealers stood dutifully in the middle of the round tables, wearing white shirts, black pants with black suspenders and black bow ties.

After an hour or so, Father would call me on my cellphone to check how I was doing, whether I had enough to eat. I always said, 'yes, the food was delicious, have you eaten?' Later, he would say, uproarious laughter ringing in the background. 'Why don't you go back now and accompany your mother? Do you have the room key with you?'

So I would walk across the casino hallways by myself, hobbling in my slightly-too-large heels, through the glass doors, past the lions and the dragons, into the gilded elevator. I would hum as the elevator swooshed several levels down, creating uncomfortable pressure in my ear tunnels. It opened with a *ding*, and I walked along the hotel corridor, also carpeted, but with a coarser, taupe material. I tapped my room card on our room's door handle and it blinked green.

Mother was inside on the King-sized bed, in pitch-black darkness, save for the blue glow on the television screen. She was wrapped in layers of white linen blankets, her eyes reflected changing scenes that she was not seeing.

'What are you watching?' I asked.

Silence. She said, 'Where is your father?'

'He's still playing. We bumped into Uncle Tan earlier. He said something about his prostate cancer being in remission now.'

She did not respond.

I would wash my face in the sink, the water smelled of perfumed chlorine. I changed into a fresh pair of pyjamas and moved into my own room through the connecting door. The rest of the night usually ended uneventfully, with me sleeping with an open book and Mother falling asleep in front of the TV. Father never returned before the break of the dawn.

It was Sunday morning and I rose early to have a morning swim in the ocean. The rolling, salty water tingled all over my skin, engulfing me in a cooling embrace. My back felt warm from the bright morning sun rays. I stretched and kicked and swam back and forth from the shoreline to the deeper part of the ocean, at the border where the line of safety buoys bobbed up and down.

There was no one else around, save for an elderly couple in the distance, holding hands under their gigantic lollipop umbrella, pink as lobsters. I had a sharp pang of a vision of my own parents sitting there, holding hands. They never held hands.

I swam for almost an hour before returning to the shore and gathered my belongings. I wrung the last drops of salt water out of my hair and turned my face against the sun. This was a good life.

'Fancy living like this for another year, eh?' Zaneta's laughing voice tinkled behind me. I turned around. She was descending the stone pathway on the embankment that led to the beach. I saw my wet face on the reflection of her sunglasses. It looked bright and happy.

'I wouldn't mind,' I reached out to get the bottle of mixed fruit juice she brought along, unscrewed the cap and drank three big gulps. 'If only Covert is not part of the package . . .'

'Still, even now, Cassie?' She shook her head disparagingly. 'How long would you need to warm up to him ...?'

'Probably, never?' I squeezed my eyes shut. The sun was getting strong. 'I'm really not sure Zane, I'm not sure how you could do anything sexual with him . . .'

'Hey, he is nice. He is really *really* nice.'

I shrugged.

'When we first met each other, you know what he told me?'

'What.'

'He said he's seen my *heart*. He said it's kind, and it's good, and that's why he fell in love with me.'

'He told you he fell in love with you? What about Margie?'

'What about her?' She passed. 'Can't he fall in love with new people?'

'Yes he can . . . it just does not make sense then that he still wants to die.'

Zaneta did not respond. She held out her hand for me to squeeze back.

'Hey, babe. Do you trust me?'

I looked at her. The same irresistible pair of green eyes, they were ablaze in the colour of deep emerald today, as if set on fire.

'Do. You. Trust. Me?'

I leaned forward and touched her lips gingerly with mine. That was the second time I had kissed her.

'More than I trust myself.'

'Then you'd need to start trusting Covert too,' She pinched my left cheek. 'Alright?'

* * *

Late afternoon, I was lying on the sofa with a book on my lap. It said *101 Rules to Cross Pollinating and Gardening*. It had a lot of glossy pictures of variegated leaf plants inside. I did not care about gardening, but it was the only coffee table book I could find, and I did not know what to do with myself. Zaneta went to the drugstore with Covert to grab some supplies. I figured probably this was how retirement felt like.

They came back rattling keys and chatter close to dinner time. Zaneta unloaded her shopping bags on the counter and started putting food and things into the freezer. Bread, milk, butter, fruits, cucumber. 'Honey bun. How's your day been?' Covert came over and pecked my cheek. Zaneta's eyes followed me. I held myself. I did not wince.

'We've been invited by the Warrens over next door for a late-night party,' Covert announced. 'Would you care to join?'

The Warrens were the couple I spotted at the beach just now, they were retired, and they were close to Covert's age. They lived in a seaside three-floor bungalow about fifteen minutes' walk from Covert's apartment.

'Party? What is it going to be like?'

'It's a private party dear,' Zaneta rinsed a good number of potatoes in the sink and left them to dry. 'You'll see later. The Warrens are so much fun.'

I thought back to their pink limbs, resting catatonically on their folding beach chairs.

'I'm not sure . . .' I looked around the room. 'I have this book I would like to finish . . .'

Even as I uttered the words, I realized how unconvincing they sounded. Neither of my options sounded interesting. Socializing with a couple of septuagenarians in a private party sounded as equally unappealing as flipping through *101 Rules to Cross Pollinating and Gardening*. I wanted excitement, energy, I wanted youth! I thought again to myself that it must be quite a miserable existence to accompany Covert for one full year at one of the retirement hotspots in the country.

Zaneta poured herself a serving of gin and tonic on clinking ice cubes. 'Tell you what. We'll head over first. When and *if* you get bored, feel free to follow us later.'

'Bonnie is going to come along too,' Covert added with passion. 'It is going to be ... E—P—I—C!'

The two of them did not stay any longer for dinner. The Warrens were throwing a seafood barbeque on their back porch. Free flow of drinks and snacks and ice cream on the house.

I started to think perhaps I was being unnecessarily difficult. *What's wrong with me? Why couldn't I be more like Zaneta or Bonnie?*

I dreamt of watching a dying bonfire up close. The dancing flames fascinated me, and I inched closer and closer so that I could feel its glaring, frenzied heat on my skin, yet as I did, I became paralysed. My smile froze on my face, my fingers knotted into an awkward configuration. 'Stoke the fire, girl! What are you doing—just standing there? Do something!' Someone behind me shouted. But I kept watching the fire without moving, I kept smiling without words. Amidst the riot of reddish—orange tongues, I saw a stack of human bones, neatly packed on top of the kindling firewood. Inside, I felt like screaming.

I opened my eyes and saw the hands on the clock pointing to half past nine in the evening. I had dozed off on the sofa, the coffee table book neglected by my side.

I felt a pang of hunger, and proceeded to the fridge to fix myself a plate of peanut butter and jelly sandwiches. I envisioned fresh barbecued prawns and stingrays as I chewed on my dry crumbling bread. Perhaps it was a mistake to turn down the Warrens' party invite. Zaneta had posted a small note on the fridge, it said: *Come over whenever you feel like it! We are going to be out till late!*

Outside, the moon glowed proud and bright like a round silver plate. I weighed my options: chewing another piece of bread and flipping through TV channels until I fell asleep drooling again or braving myself to a round of laughter and cheers with the retirees and Zaneta and Bonnie.

To hell with it. Let's just go with the flow. I took one of Covert's bottles of liquor from the shelf, tilted it above my mouth and poured the burning amber liquid into my throat. I supposed that was whiskey. I wiped my mouth on my sleeve, grabbed the spare keys and walked out into the windy beach.

The sand still felt warm in between my toes as I trudged towards the Warrens' bungalow. I saw the darkened silhouette of their cabin in the distance, a singular yellow light glowing dimly against the velvety black of the night. It looked eerily quiet.

The wind whistled in high notes in my ear, it was warm and dry, and I felt completely defenseless. I was wearing a halter top and frayed shorts, my hair tied in a high ponytail, like a classic small town American sweetheart. Sometimes I felt taken aback at how foreign I had become to myself. One moment I would close my eyes and see the old me, sitting primly in front of my school's chapel in Jakarta, waiting for my driver in my red-and-white uniform. And then I'd open them and here I was, deflecting sand out of my eyes, standing in front of a retired couple's beach house, on a curious spring break sugar dating gig set by my semi-lesbian *femme fatale* of a girlfriend. This was America, and everything was possible.

The Warrens' house remained dead silent. I pressed my ear against the smooth wooden door, for any sign of thumping, beats of music, or whatever else. I got nothing. I knocked several times. Nothing still.

'Hello?' I started. 'Covert? Zaneta? Bonnie? Is anyone there . . .?'

I counted back sixty seconds and turned the door handle. It opened effortlessly. I had passed by their back porch twice by now, every time their French doors were wide open to reveal the kitchen inside, and it always looked sleek and modern and bright with polished countertops and silver-plated refrigerators and sparkling wine glasses hanging above the shelves. That night though, the kitchen was completely dark and uninviting from the inside.

'Guys? Is there anyone here?'

There was only one light being turned on inside the house, at the foyer, which was the singular light I saw from the distance.

I felt my way towards the dark kitchen, stumbled upon a switch and turned it on, blinking several times to adjust my vision. Plates of leftover food crowded the island. I saw grilled fish, prawn, lobster, corn and vegetables. There were numerous bags of chips loitering around. The sink was filled with stained glasses. I smelled wine and soda.

So they were here eating. Where could they possibly be now? I went up the staircase and checked on the bedrooms.

There was no one, there was no sound. I went back down, eyeing the tasteful interior, the rows of framed photographs of the Warrens with their children and grandchildren, as if I could find any clues there.

Finally I saw a door by the pantry that was slightly ajar, opening to darkness. I did not know that they had a basement. I pulled down the cord switch and it buzzed overhead, lighting up the steep stairs leading down. There was a row of washing machines at the foot of the stairs, and behind them, another door. It was huge and completely padded, like a soundproof door to a bunker.

I pressed my ear on the leather pads, and at long last, caught some muffled voices. Thank God. I gave the door a push, expecting it to be locked, but it gave way effortlessly to my weight.

There was a flood of warm yellow hues, streaming from a crystal chandelier above my head. Soft jazzy tunes crackled from an old record player at the corner. In the middle of the room was a huge fluffy poster bed. Flesh-toned figures shifted and swayed on top of a red silk bedspread.

'Faster, baby, faster . . .'

Someone was moaning like an animal.

For a moment my brain failed to register what my eyes were seeing. I saw Covert first. His face strained into a senseless grin, appearing flusher than usual from his exertion. I saw the constellation of liver spots on his skin, dotted with beads of sweat. Bonnie was on all fours, her bum before him. Her milky white breasts seemingly of outsized proportion, hanging heavy from her ribcage. She shook steadily as Covert thumped into her. In front of her, Zaneta was kneeling stark naked like a bronze statue. Her back arching deep, one hand combed through her curls, Bonnie's face in between her thighs. She sighed profusely, a dreamy smile spread over her lips.

I saw the Warrens having sex to the left of the threesome. Their old, bent bodies contorted impressively, sags, fats, wrinkles and all tangled up into a big hot mess.

Covert looked up, and his eyes lighted up with a new flash of desire. 'Ahhh, look who's here . . .'

He pulled out of Bonnie and flipped her over so that her stomach faced him. Her breasts were two big dangling pears that fell to her sides.

Zaneta opened her eyes and looked at me dreamily. She reclined back on her elbows, smiling and watching lazily.

'You came just in time . . .' Covert clapped. 'For dessert!'

The Warrens did not stop. They looked up momentarily and gave me a smile of acknowledgement. Mrs Warren looked frail and bird-like, her hair as thin as cotton candy and her face looked like she was in pain. With every jerk, I feared that she would break something critical, but nothing of the sort had happened. Mr Warren looked slightly sturdier. His stomach spilled towards his pointy knees, and he was grinning ear to ear as he went in and out of his wife.

'Come, my love,' Zaneta extended her shapely fingers. Her gaze was steady, almost hypnotic.

I did not want to get closer, yet somehow, I did.

Covert grabbed Bonnie's left breast, put his mouth over the nipple. He sucked hard while she whimpered. He looked up and smacked his lips, his moustache covered in white.

'Try it, Cutie Pie. It is delicious,' he gestured at me.

I did not want to move forward, yet I did, again. Zaneta's gaze bore down at my nape. At this point it just felt increasingly exhausting to keep pushing back.

I looked down at Bonnie. Her cheeks flushed red with delight. She seemed genuinely happy.

'May I?'

She held up her right breast. 'It's all yours babe.'

Her nipple was overly pointed with a ring of decidedly dark areola. I stooped forward, inserted the rubber-like button in between my lips, and sucked. A gush of thick, warm fluid filled my throat. I held my breath and swallowed. It tasted like pungent butter, almost sweet.

I looked up and wiped my mouth.

'How was it, eh?' Covert chuckled delightfully.

'That was nice. Thank you.' I looked at Zaneta.

'I left . . . my phone at home . . . I think I need to go, if that's alright.'

'Of course Sweetheart. Thanks for dropping by.'

She blew me a kiss.

I waited until I was outside the bungalow before I started running as fast as I could. I ran towards the high tide. Once my ankles reached the warm, raging water, I bent over and puked everything out. I puked and puked, I could feel the remnants of my peanut butter and jelly sandwich went out into the sea. I puked until I trembled like a leaf. The water reached all the way up to my thighs.

When I was finally done, my face was wet with tears.

Chapter Seven

My Disneyland Romance

It was not that I had been a prude throughout my time in the United States, before this curious arrangement with Covert began. Sex was never a scarce commodity at Harvard. Young, attractive, intellectual, raging with adolescent hormones, my esteemed college mates never failed to come up with the most inventive schemes of lovemaking, on a weekly basis. Come Thursday, after the last classes ended, the college dormitories officially turned into a rowdy adult playground where cheap beer in plastic red cups fuelled dark, sweaty, parties in numerous living rooms of the upper-class men's flats.

Starting sophomore year, I moved out of my freshman dormitory into Mather House, proudly occupying the ugliest buildings in the whole campus, with its concrete brutalist architecture and old musty carpet from the seventies smelling like cat's pee.

Mather was famous for being the 'cheap party' house, our gem event-of-the-year being Mather Lather, where our high-ceilinged, glass-walled dining room turned into a public foam pit glamourized with changing-colour portable disco balls. Rumours had it that the suds from the foam machine gave you skin rashes, but it did not seem to stop everyone far and wide across campus to come and willfully lather themselves with the said irritants.

Students wearing skimpy bikinis and tiny thongs and creative body paint happily glided against each other to the latest beats of someone's YouTube pop playlist blasting from the speakers. After the whole affair concluded, guests of roommates flocked to all our bathrooms to take showers, separately, and more often together. I remembered locking myself faithfully in my room to rush a mid-term anthropology paper on Durkheim that I had struggled to finish, and sneaking out to my co-ed bathroom to brush my teeth, only to stumble upon naked six-pack torsos and bouncing breasts covered in nipple plasters. Every corner I looked, people seemed to be engaged in complicated space-saving contortions, kissing and slobbering all over each other amidst the suffocating steam from the showers.

'How's your night going so far?'

A six-feet-tall, beefy kid grinned at me from ear to ear as I squeezed my toothpaste onto my toothbrush. I turned to face his hairy chest. 'Night's going great . . . Thank you. How's yours?'

'Couldn't be better.' He stretched his arms above his head and scratched at his armpit. 'Do you live here?'

'Yes, this is my unit.'

'Did you like the foam party? What do you think?'

'Actually . . .' I started, and changed my mind. 'Wow yeah, that was sick. Highlight of the year!'

'I know, right??' He looked like he could be a quarterback on our football team.

'Where are you from?'

'Indonesia. Where are you from?'

'Mississippi.' His torso moved, the ripples of his chest signalled equal parts muscles and fat. 'You know . . . I've never known anyone from Indonesia before.'

His eyes looked open and friendly, like that of a golden retriever.

'I see.'

'Have you hung out with anyone from Mississippi before?'

'No, not really. Isn't it a river?'

'Well yeah, it's a state. But also, a river.'

'Interesting.'

A pause, and then, I heard myself say, 'What would you like to know about Indonesians?'

Half an hour later, the football player was pushing into me from behind, against the walls of my tiny dormitory room. He was thumping over and over with the formidable force of a bull, everything about his body was thick and angular. I had never felt dirtier and cheaper, yet this derogatory self-perception only made me come even harder and faster. After he relieved himself, he burped loudly and left the room with a sheepish grin. I continued my paper and submitted the whole draft by the break of dawn. It received an A from my professor.

Indeed, Mather Lather was one of the best examples of creative debauchery Harvard had to offer, perhaps followed closely by Incest Fest at Kirkland, the house next door, a private affair where the residents of the house were encouraged to familiarize themselves with each other under rotten circumstances. 'It was always an awkward moment in the morning after, when we saw everyone again having breakfast in the morning,' my friend Luis, a junior at Kirkland told me. 'But hey, that was part of the ethos. After Incest Fest, you are officially a Kirklander.'

Sex in The Stacks was another thing you had to tick off your college bucket list. Widener library was the place to do it, being the oldest and biggest library in the whole campus. It was stately and imposing, with an expanse of wide steps leading to a row of gargantuan Corinthian columns that fronted its red-brick façade. The whole building had stacks and stacks of dense bookshelves that extended via a tunnel into a three-level underground library (the 'Pusey Library', as it happened to be called.) It was the kind of library that you would get lost in.

Junior year in college, I matched with a graduate student from the Kennedy school on Tinder and right off the bat he requested for a venture into the stacks.

I hesitated.

'It would be an honour to do this with you,' the man solemnly declared. Steve was blonde and blue eyed with handsome square jaws. He served for the Green Berets in the Middle East and was planning to run for congress after his degree. 'As you see, I need you to do this, as Sex in The Stacks is a college tradition, and not a Kennedy school tradition . . . We need to respect tradition.'

His sincerity touched me. I never thought that seriously about Sex in The Stacks, let alone went out of my way to find a willing partner to do this specifically, but maybe I should have. After all, the onus was on me as an attending college student to preserve tradition.

'Alright. Let's do it.'

Steve took charge of the whole thing with the discipline, determination, and precision of a military operation. He instructed that we meet at the 2100 hour to the east side of the library and enter separately. I was to walk in first and headed straight to the Pusey Library level two and waited for Steve near the entrance for exactly fifteen minutes.

'This was great timing, when things would have become quieter in the library. The danger, of course, was that the remaining few attendants would be making a move to leave during this time and anyone might run into us. Hence, we should explore far into the depths of the stacks. I'd propose . . . we went under stealth mode to the section about the ecclesiastical art of the thirteenth century . . . that should be one of the least visited collections of books, don't you think so babe?'

I frowned and thought about it for a full three minutes, so it would appear that I was making an equal contribution to the planning. 'How about neo shamanic rituals in Latin America . . . I think that should be quite niche too . . .'

'Babe, are you kidding me? That is the stuff of ayahuasca and psychedelics. Kids these days are crazy about those!'

'You're right. Let's stick to ecclesiastical art.'

At precisely 9 p.m. that night, we met beside the library building. Steve had a stocky build and he walked with an almost mechanical gait, foot marching forward at a time. He carried a backpack with him and set his phone on a timer. 'I have a video camcorder here and a tripod to record the whole thing . . . and some ski masks, if you'd like to cover your face? Condoms, lubricants . . .' he chuckled and pulled out a handcuff, 'And even some toys if we need better visuals but totally up to you darling. I think the library background in itself is enough stimulation.'

I came in my hoodie and pyjama bottoms and uggs boots carrying nothing but my student ID card. It was early autumn, and the weather was fairly chilly.

'Alright, ready?'

I nodded. 'Good luck.'

I went into the library and headed straight to the front desk. 'I need to get some books from the Pusey Library.'

The librarian glanced at the clock and looked back at me. She motioned with her hand, 'That way, just tap your card.'

I tapped my card at one machine among the rows of gates leading to the back door and it blinked green. I tapped one more time at the door and it clicked open. Inside the tunnel, it was cool and dark with linoleum flooring and brick walls. I took the stairs down to the second level and waited by the first shelf. There were tables in the open area before the stacks began, and there were only three students sitting there, typing away at their laptops.

Exactly fifteen minutes later Steve showed up as promised. He winked at me and I could feel my desire build up. We avoided touching each other and walked side by side about eighteen shelves down the corridor and turned to the target section. Rows and rows of dusty hardcover books embossed in gold and silver towered over us.

Steve looked around to check that no one was in our vicinity. He set up his tripod, camera and pressed on his timer. 'We have thirty minutes.' He threw one ski mask at me and wore one himself. I considered it for a while but shook my head eventually. 'I think I want my face to show for this.'

I could see a big grin forming behind his mask. In one firm motion he pushed me on my knees to face the camera and yanked my hair. He reached forward and pressed the record button. I looked right into the lens, meeting eye to eye with an imaginary audience.

Steve breathed urgently on my neck. 'This is so hot, babe.'

He helped me out of my hoodie and pyjama pants and boots, down to my plain bras and undies. He was not taking off his shirt, but I heard him struggle with his belt. Within minutes, I felt his penis pressing into my naked butt, and he slipped it right past my underwear. I was so wet I almost came with the first thrust.

Steve continued pushing deeper and deeper. We settled into a mechanical rhythm, not unlike his walking gait. I rolled my eyes back into my head and sighed and moaned as enticingly as I could.

I thought I saw footsteps around the corner, but I could not be sure of it. The idea gave me thrilling goosebumps.

The alarm buzzed off. Steve pulled out and stroked himself in front of my face. 'Almost . . . Almost . . . Ready?'

I nodded.

He relieved himself into my mouth. I closed my eyes and swallowed whole. Steve shuddered dramatically and gave a loud sigh. He turned off the camera and packed everything neatly back into his backpack. I brushed dust and particles off my skin and got back into my clothes clumsily. Meanwhile, there was no interruption whatsoever to Steve's chain of actions, one followed each other like clockwork.

'I have trained well, babe. There was no time to lose in the warzone,' he said, as if he could read my mind. 'Now . . . I'll go out and head home first. You'll go out exactly at ten, alright, when the library closes? You should sit first and pretend to read.'

I did as he said. We never linked up again, and I never saw the footage that he took. Nevertheless, I maintained that Sex in the Stacks was one of the most memorable sex experiences I had had in my life to this day.

'We are going to Disneyland,' Covert announced on Monday. He was wearing round, dark glasses, a polo cap, a polo shirt and Bermuda shorts.

Zaneta yelped in excitement. I looked up from my book. I was halfway through reading *The Notebook* as a case study for a codependent relationship. 'Did you hear that Cassie? Disneyland Orlando is awesome!'

'Sure,' I said. 'I love roller coasters. Is Bonnie going to join again?'

'No, just us. Just us.' Covert petted the top of my head. I had managed to stay completely still now whenever he touched me. However, after what happened at the Warren's, I would be glad to never see Bonnie ever again.

I loved amusement parks. I loved getting lost in the fun mirror house and jumping onboard all sorts of rides. I loved drop towers and roller coasters, carousels and Ferris wheels. I loved licking on cotton candy and had it melted into sand underneath my tongue. I'd love to go to an amusement park with Zaneta, but I wasn't sure that Covert would be fit to jump on any ride.

'I'm good with carousels . . . And themed rides perhaps,' Covert said, as if he could read my mind.

I closed my book. 'Alright, what should we bring?' I went into my room and grabbed a small carry-on. I started packing sunscreen, sunhat, sunglasses, and a water bottle. I threw my mobile phone in. I did not carry any wallet with me, it was a given that Covert took care of all our expenses during this trip.

Ali did not pick us up this time round. Covert took out his white Volkswagen from the parking lot and ignited the engine. Zaneta flashed her brilliant grin as she stepped into the shotgun seat. 'What are we waiting for? I'm ready to go!'

The drive to Orlando took around two hours via the highway. The hot sun set ablaze in the expanse of bright blue sky above. I reclined in the back seat of the car, my feet put up against the windowpane. I had my sunglasses on. Buildings and palm trees blurred past one after another in sepia colour behind my shaded vision.

We drove for what felt like a long time. Zaneta was playing 'I Spy' with Covert in front. Her childlike enthusiasm was simultaneously charming and puzzling. I was not sure where all her energy came from, but I was grateful that I was spared the obligation to entertain anyone.

When we finally arrived, it was lunch time. Covert bought us tickets and we went straight to a Snow-White themed restaurant. Zaneta ordered ice cream, cookies and pizza. They came in with little plastic dwarfs attached to them, and sweet lemon iced tea served in gigantic colourful mugs.

I chewed on the pizza and licked the ice cream slowly. Everything was cheesy, rich and buttery sweet that it cloyed my senses after a few bites.

'Let's get to the rides.' I announced.

We went to Seaworld and took the roller coaster ride. Covert dutifully sat and waited outside, guarding our bags. Zaneta threw her hands up in the air and screamed from on top of her lungs while I squinted my eyes and scrunched my face. We went into the funhouse, doing weird poses in the mirrors and taking tons of pictures with our mobile phones. We tried more thrilling adventure themed rides and simulation rides. We dressed up as Disney's princess and took pictures with Disney characters. This proved to be Zaneta favourite activities. She tried on all the costumes from *The Little Mermaid* to Jasmine to Cinderella and Elsa from *Frozen*. I got my cotton candy in pastel yellow and blue and pink and sucked on it happily. Covert watched over us like a happy parent, his moustache twitching with joy.

There was something generous and sweet about Covert. He complained about prices from time to time, however I could tell that he genuinely cared about our well-being and he brightened up when we asked for and received his gifts.

He appreciated touching and being touched. Often I found his fingers tracing the back of my neck, down to my lower back, or removing a strand of hair behind my ear. I tried my best to return his affection with smiles and eyes sparkly with appreciation, but I could never bring myself to touch him back. Zaneta on the other hand, had no problem massaging his neck, hugging him from behind, resting her head on his shoulders, holding his hand while they walked together as if they were a loving couple. I never saw them kiss, not even at The Warren's, so I supposed it was something that she reserved for Blake.

We sauntered over to the arcade games. There was a basketball ring and Covert proved to be quite the player. Zaneta encouraged him from the side, clapping her hands in delight every single time Covert scored. He never missed, not even once. He won a huge decorated plush unicorn for Zaneta and got me a golden covered pocketbook.

I watched Covert carry the unicorn into the car. He walked with a more erect posture, open chest, open smile and reddish cheeks. I never noticed that he had sea green-blue eyes, a little bit cloudish from early signs of cataract forming, but in that hour under the bright Orlando sun, they shone in vivid colours. He threw his head back and shook with a full-belly laughter. I thought to myself that I had never seen anyone happier but Zaneta. She did good for him.

Zaneta told us that she was going to queue for the bathroom, so we waited together on the bench outside. Covert fidgeted beside me, offering to buy a bottle of lemonade or a bag of candy.

'I had a good time today. Thanks,' I reassured him.

He stayed quiet for a while.

'You know . . . it matters to me that you feel good and feel taken care of. You should let me know if you ever want or need anything. I know exactly what Zaneta wants, she always asks. But I'm not very sure about your needs or your wants . . .'

I was not sure either.

'Don't beat yourself up. I wish I could be as free and certain of myself as she is.'

'She is really something special, isn't she?' Covert gazed into the distance. 'I have never felt like this for anyone before.'

She did have that effect on everyone, including me. Nevertheless, I felt a pang of jealousy, of feeling less of her worth. I doubted that anyone would ever say the same about me, no matter how hard I tried to be someone out of this world. How someone could make you feel both superior and inferior was beyond me. I felt magnified in her presence, yet I knew that when she turned away, my light would dim, and everybody would as soon forget that I was there.

'How about Margie?' I heard myself say, almost as if I was offended. 'Did you not also feel powerfully for her?'

Covert looked at me with intent. 'Well. Zaneta is like no one else, don't you agree?'

A pause and then, 'She unlocked things I didn't know were within me.'

'Okay. I get that.'

We sat for a while under the setting sun, an orange yolk on the horizon.

I counted a few seconds before asking. 'Are you sure that you are ready to quit . . . this life . . .?'

'That was my promise to her. I would not go back on what I said.'

I waited a while again. 'Is it even . . . legal? To help with this kind of thing?'

Covert drew a long breath. 'No, I'm afraid not.'

'I saw in the papers last time about this girl who was helping with his boyfriend's suicide. I think she had to serve some time in prison . . . It was in Massachusetts.'

Covert did not respond.

'And I mean, with inheritance of *that* significance, I think it would be even harder to get away without causing a lot of probing. There are just so many . . . things that would go *seriously* wrong.'

Covert stared ahead.

'Ten million,' he finally said. 'Excuse me, what?'

'Ten million, I can promise you that much if you'd help me. And twenty for her. Everything I have.'

I could not even imagine living a life with that much purchasing power.

'Today you seem so . . . *happy*. I'm not sure that you are done with everything . . . Just yet.'

'Within a year I will,' he said. 'And can't I be both ecstatic and depressed at once? Can't I find life as equally magnificent as I find it insufferable?'

'That was a very good point.'

Zaneta appeared shortly after and instinctively I kept my mouth shut. I thought that she would not be happy if she knew I was asking more problematic questions.

It was a good day. We drove back home covered in sweat and the sticky sweetness of ice cream and cotton candy on our skin.

I slept my whole way back to Jensen Beach. Zaneta rested her head on my shoulder and snored gently all the way through.

I took a sharp breath and opened my eyes in alarm. My phone glowed in the dark, showing 12:33 a.m. We got back home at around 9 p.m. and I went straight to bed. I wasn't sure why I'd woken up so abruptly.

Zaneta was still fast asleep beside me. I had moved out of Covert's room after the first night and camped in her room. I was thankful that no one questioned me.

The whole penthouse was dark and quiet, save for a single lightbulb in the kitchen. I heard Covert snoring in the next room. My tongue felt rubbery and tasted like lead. I poured a tall glass of water from the tap and drank it quickly.

I needed a cigarette.

I reached into the drawer by the front door and pulled out a cigarette and a lighter. I never bought any myself, to keep my consumption in check, however I would look for a smoke from time to time. I shoved the cigarette, the lighter, and a set of keys into my jeans' pocket and took the elevator down.

It was dark outside, but the beach was brightly lit under the moon. I inhaled several deep long breaths and walked to a raised embankment several metres from the shoreline. The lull of the ocean brought me to a state of calm. I sat on a rock and lit my cigarette, staring at the dark waves lapping forward and backward over the sand.

I was not sure how much time passed by just like so, suspended in my hazy contemplation. I was thinking about how odd the trajectory of human lives was, all the places we could go, all the people we could meet, all the stories we ended up weaving for ourselves, stranger than fiction, dreamier than fairytales.

Someone touched me on my shoulders, and I almost jumped. 'What, the hell!'

'Whoa, I'm sorry, I didn't mean to scare you . . .' A platinum-haired boy with icy blue eyes, both of his palms facing outwards in a gesture intended to calm me down. The boy was so pale I could almost see blue veins underneath his overstretched skin, even in the dim moonlight. He was an albino.

'I thought I saw someone smoking here. I just wanted to say hello,' he shrugged.

'Hello.'

He looked somewhat amused. 'I'm Seth. Seth Longcroft' he offered his hand. 'I live in my parents' basement, right over there.'

I almost choked on my smoke. 'You—what?'

'Well I'm a startup founder, you see . . . I'm bootstrapping.'

'Alright.'

'Do you have any more cigarettes with you?'

'No, sorry, actually this is the only one I brought with me.'

'Actually it's fine. I don't have to smoke.'

He sat down, right next to me, his thigh touching mine without misgiving. His skin was cold and papery, and his presence was light but grounded. I saw the contour of his lean stature moved and rippled under the shadows of the palm trees. He looked at once fragile and resolute.

'Tell me about this startup then. What do you claim to be building?'

The boy chuckled. 'That's how bad the reputation of startup founders is these days, eh?'

I shrugged. 'Too much money. Too little value.'

'We can only dream of greatness though.'

'Or win the lottery.'

He laughed again, deep and bold.

'I'm building something on the blockchain. Something like, peer to peer lending protocol. I mean now we are bootstrapping, but soon we'll be launching our tokens, so that's like an instant IPO, and if prices go up . . .'

'That is going to be the time to exit?' I offered.

He looked at me. 'I'm not like that.'

'Sure, nobody is *like* that.'

He stood up and his eyes shone like a pair of blue sapphires. 'No, I'm serious. If there's one thing you need to know about me now . . . I am a man of principles.'

'You know, you don't need to care what I think of you.'

He sat again, hunched and smiling. 'You're right. I want to though . . .'

'Want what?'

'Want to care about what you think of me.'

'You don't even know my name.'

'What's your name?'

I tried to look offended yet burst out laughing at once. 'Cassandra. Cassandra Lie Setiawan.'

'What's that?'

'Just call me Cassie. You won't be able to remember it.'

'You're not from here, are you? I heard a little bit of an accent.'

'You are right. I'm from Indonesia. Well, Singapore too.'

'How's it over there?'

'Hot.'

'Hotter than here?'

'Hotter. Humid. The heat is almost punishing.'

'I'd like to go visit. One day.'

'Everybody says that. Not everybody would do it.'

'Watch me.'

We laughed again, together now. I was not sure how to describe how I felt about this kid. I felt somewhat wittier and funnier around him, and that was unusual.

'So what are you doing here, Cassie? All the way from tropical islands, cast in Martin County, Florida, of all places?

'I can't tell you Seth. You'd be having the shock of your life if you figured it out.'

'Let me guess . . . some kind of sorority spring break trip?'

'Yeah actually, something like that.'

Sorority of the sugar babies for the millions. Three members pledged—me, Zaneta, Bonnie.

'Where do you go to school?'

'Harvard.'

I said it without a moment's hesitation, as if it was the most correct thing to say, because indeed it was the truth. However, it usually took me great hesitation to tell people about where I went to school, simply because I did not want anyone to have any unwarranted assumption about me.

Seth whistled. 'I knew you were smart.'

'And lucky.'

'Don't play it down.'

'Alright, I'm smart.'

It felt good, talking to him. I had never felt more at ease with myself.

'How long are you going to be here for?'

'Well until the end of spring break . . . Which is about six more days . . . But I might be back. For a year.'

He tilted his head. 'Really? What for?'

'I told you I can't tell you.'

I could tell that Seth finally digested this information thoroughly. 'So you weren't joking.'

'No I wasn't.'

'Everyone is entitled to their own secret.'

'I know that, but thanks for reminding me of *my* rights.'

'Maybe you'd tell me before the end of the week.'

'Maybe. Nothing is impossible.'

We sat in silence for a while, it was a kind of silence that ensconced you in knowing comfort. Nothing needed to be said to sustain this delicate balance. I wanted to tell him that, but at the same time I knew I did not have to.

'I think I needed to go back to bed,' I finally said. 'Will I be seeing you around?'

'What are you doing tomorrow?'

'I can make myself available.'

Seth stood up and offered his hand again to help me rise to my feet. 'Alright, deal. Let's meet here tomorrow, say lunch time? I want to take you to a place.'

'Sounds good.'

He was shaking his head, smiling. 'You reminded me of someone, someone I knew . . . from a long time ago. When I was a little boy, there was this girl who came to my neighbourhood with her diplomat parents. She was either from Thailand or Malaysia . . .'

'Please don't be racist. Don't ruin our moment.'

He was laughing one last time. I winked at him and turned around, walking right back to Covert's apartment. For the first time since moving to America, I had a glimpse of what it would be like to be Zaneta, and actually meant it.

Chapter Eight

A Woman Who Had It All

Right before my last spring break in Florida that year with Zaneta and Covert, a week-long sugaring arrangement fell into my lap with a patron from *Strings Attached*. His name was David Huntley and he was attached to The Pentagon in conjunction with his role as a director for the National Security Council. He owned a security and policy consulting company, and a few construction companies building roads and infrastructure in war-torn Middle Eastern regions, incorporated in Delaware. He was making a good living for himself and his family, and then some.

David reached out to me in a politely written message. At forty-five, I thought that he looked a little bit like a moustachioed, unfit version of Bruce Willis in the 2013 *Die Hard* movie. He was an alumnus, he studied politics and history. He had a picture of himself skydiving, and another picture of him hugging two pink-cheeked adolescent daughters in front of a Christmas tree. It said on his profile that he was separated from his wife, and they were co-raising their kids together.

'I'd like to take you to the Top of The Hub for a nice lunch. You seem interesting, I like your energy. How would you like that?'

I had been to Top of The Hub only once during my freshman year. It was a historic fancy dining restaurant, with a 360-degree panoramic view of Greater Boston through floor-to-ceiling glass walls. I went there with Becky, my Korean roommate and we both ordered a glass of wine because that was the only thing we could afford, while watching the red sunset over skyscrapers turned into a silver round moon. We put on nice little dresses and pretended that the staff did not pay attention that we were sipping our wine for a good four hours.

'I'd like to have a date at The Top of The Hub, I've never been!' I worried that I might sound too eager, but if I learnt anything from my college dating life now, it was that men did not bother to put any effort anymore. Thanks to the convenience of online dating and hookup culture, it seemed to me that gentlemanly gestures had been dead and gone for generations to come.

'Perfect! Shall we set a time and date then? I could send an Uber over to pick you up.' The answer came immediately. I did not have to play games. It was a breath of fresh air.

I found myself sitting face to face with the gentleman from Washington DC on a small round table next to the window at The Top of The Hub. It was a bright Sunday afternoon. He was a little bit portlier than his pictures but nevertheless his eagle-sharp green eyes radiated a sort of magnetic intensity that drew me in.

'What has your Harvard experience been like?' He poured me a glass of rosé wine.

'It has been great so far. I couldn't complain. I could study practically anything under the sun.'

'Funny. I didn't feel like that. I had a goal to work in politics and I knew what was fit for studying . . . certainly I did not feel like I had the freedom that you had.'

'I was doing fieldwork on neo-shamanic communities in the West Coast, and wrote a paper about the communal spirit and culture of Burning Man.' I elaborated. 'And last semester I went to the island Exuma in the Bahamas to collect qualitative data on green urban planning with the GSD school.'

He chuckled. 'I envy you.'

'No need to be envious,' I said, sipping on my wine. 'I'd be lucky to make a quarter of what you make in this lifetime.'

He ordered a big, boiled lobster with lemon and spices for me, as I requested, with beetroot salad and shrimp avocado cocktails. There was an unlimited supply of bread and butter and fruity wine. I was impressed.

By the end of lunch we were giggly and lightheaded from the alcohol. David put his hand on top of mine, and I felt a surge of fondness.

'I like you.'

I nodded my head.

'Listen, I'm gonna be here for about a week . . . to meet some business partners and attend an alumni networking event. Would you like to consider a week-long arrangement? Maybe if things work well we could have a longer term arrangement.'

It was very direct and clear cut. There were no confusing boundaries, no conflicting signals. He laid all his cards on the table. It felt natural for me to say yes. We agreed on eight grand for the whole week which averaged on one grand per day. That was more money than I could ever expect from a full-time job after graduation.

I liked David. Not in an infatuated, possessive way, more like an endearing sense of sweet affection. He had a lot of interesting input and a direct exposure to a world I would never gain access to in this lifetime. He was the perfect man for such an arrangement, he seemed well-versed with the terms and conditions. Money made it easy too, as it was so elegantly simple and grounding. I did not have any qualms to continue engaging with him.

In the bedroom he was equally accommodating. It was not as passionate as it was comfortable, but I gladly obliged to spend every night of that week tucked under his fluffy bed covers in a hotel downtown and took the train back to Cambridge to attend my morning classes.

He spooned me from behind every night and caressed my hair. 'You know everyone is just looking for companionship, essentially. I'm not sure why it has become such a rare commodity.'

'Yes, perhaps.'

If anything, I was looking for more time alone with myself. There was round-the-clock exposure to students and group classes and parties on campus. There was hardly time to be by myself. I constantly felt compelled to attend everything and to make the full use of my time and resources there.

'You know . . . I could connect you to some American think tank in Jakarta if you ever want to work in policy or something similar. I think anthropologists would be great for such a role.'

I did not tell him that I had very little intention to go back and work in my hometown, around my parents, but I thanked him anyway.

'I have another long-term sugar baby in North Carolina. She is a sophomore and she is very sweet.'

'I see.'

I did not feel anything at all. I barely even blinked. It was a good sign.

'What about dating properly and remarrying?' I asked.

'Well, for starters, my wife would not agree to a divorce, not until both of our daughters reached eighteen. And you know, hanging out with an older man like me might not be very exciting for sweet, young girls, but if they could get a lot of value out of it, that is a win-win for everyone. The ambitious and curious ones usually find this kind of relationship appealing.'

I did not think of myself as ambitious, but maybe he was right. I was trading affection for concrete economic benefits.

He told me that he had spent almost a million dollars on girls for the past five years, from long-term monthly payments to trips and expensive dates, luxury gifts and investments. He had engaged with everyone from high-flying prostitutes .to high-class escorts to college-aged sugar babies looking to earn extra pocket money. He helped a couple of Eastern European ladies buy properties for themselves in their hometowns. He supported a few girls through college. Some of them did not even have any sexual relationship with him, he was happy to oblige to various agreements.

I took in all of these—was I selling short somehow by having sex with David? I did want it though, it was not much of a problem. He was attractive enough, but I did wonder if I'd have sex with him without everything else on the table.

'Why would you do that?' I asked. 'Why would you not find a normal girlfriend—perhaps someone of your equal in economic stature . . . Equal in age? What's wrong with that?'

He chuckled and nuzzled my neck.

'I appreciate beauty though. I love spending on pretty little things.'

'And you've got no problem that they only appreciate you for what you gifted them, and not for *you* as a person?'

'It is a little sad if you put it that way . . . but certainly, I could argue that you genuinely appreciate my generous nature, which is innate in me? Again, what should I do? I'm a sucker for beauty. That's just the way it is, and I have accepted it.

I am certainly not complaining about being born with all the opportunities to accumulate wealth that many pretty girls like yourself won't be able to do in this lifetime. Isn't it just fair?'

That statement hit a spot in my gut, it almost felt like skinny dipping into ice-cold water. I never thought of my gender identity in the ways that made me reflect on my place on this planet and the options available for me.

What is fair? What is not fair? Everybody has a price.

Then again, if it was not the way the world was supposed to work best, why did we find ourselves settling into this current structure of power and hierarchy?

I waited at the exact same rock for Seth the next day. It looked open and inviting under the bright sunlight. I looked around, no soul was in sight, but I knew that he was somewhere around. I sat at the rock and stared at the sparkling ocean, waiting.

A hand rested gently on my shoulder. I jolted in surprise and looked at him. For a moment I suspected he had been watching and waiting until I sat down there. He'd prefer I would not know which direction he was coming from.

'How's your day with the sorority sister?'

'Not bad. Quite relaxing. They are in Orlando now,' I added. 'I bailed.'

Seth leaped onto the rock and squatted down, squinting his eyes like a feline creature. 'I'm honoured. Are you ready?'

I nodded. He led me towards the path opening to the residential area and the main road. A motorbike was standing next to a newer condominium complex. 'Here put this on,' he threw me a helmet. I fixed it on my head and hopped on the passenger seat.

He gripped and turned on the handles and the bike lurched forward, vomiting gray smoke. 'Hang tight, this baby is quite old.'

We roared through the road and turned into a small alleyway that took us to an opening with a wooden slatted jetty stretching into the ocean. There was a blue and white restaurant by the jetty, with a bunch of circular tables and seats outdoors, protected by big white-and-blue umbrellas. Seth killed the engine and offered his hand to help me dismount. I took off my helmet.

We sat down to a nice lunch of seafood, risotto and salad. Seth ordered a jug of white wine, it tasted clear and light with low alcohol content. It was nice.

I chewed on fresh shrimp, playing a little bit with my risotto. After swallowing a few mouthfuls, I drank a little bit of wine. Seth looked at me and I looked at him.

'Thank you for lunch.'

'Whoever said I was paying?'

I rolled my eyes and poured another glass. 'I'm certainly not paying. This means we need to dine and dash.'

We chuckled for a while. 'My parents had their wedding ceremony here,' Seth said. 'Some thirty years ago.'

'Really, this restaurant is that old,' I looked around. It looked just like any establishment along Jensen Beach.

'Actually, they owned this. They have some businesses.'

I laughed. 'Ah, that's the real reason you brought me here.'

He raised his hand and ordered us both a small piece of chocolate cake, with a cup of macchiato.

'I have funding, but I'd need to bootstrap until I show some returns,' he said. 'Living in the basement was not ideal, but I'm a committed founder, you see.'

'Understood.'

'It should not be too long, though. I'm excited about things that we are going to launch very soon.'

'I have no doubt.'

It was not an empty lip service, I was not doubting him. 'We are all working towards something, ain't we?'

He did not ask me what my plan was after graduation, which I found a bit odd, seeing that he shared so much about his own situation. Perhaps he was waiting for me to speak up myself.

'How are your parents? Are they . . . happy with each other?'

'Sure they do. They are very sweet with each other. They are business partners, and they work well together too. They have a few businesses together.'

'That's nice.'

'Why? What about yours?' Finally a question.

I shrugged. 'Sure. I don't know. Mom would always begrudge him.'

'That's not nice.'

'I think he has a mistress . . . On top of the karaoke girls.'

'Karaoke girls?'

'You know, they are like . . . Modern geishas. In Asia. You need them to sweeten business deals with business partners . . . In pubs and karaokes and private parties.'

Seth nodded. 'I can imagine.'

'She tolerated the karaoke girls. They are part of the package. But I sensed there was someone else, a long-term girlfriend. Perhaps I have a few more siblings I do not know.'

'Do you have any proof?'

I thought back to the buzzing, ringing phone in the hotel room in Singapore almost a decade ago, still threateningly loud even under the pillow I threw on top of it.

'Yes.' That was all I could say.

Seth did not press further. Suddenly we were playing footsie under the table and stared at each other, grinning.

'So are you going to tell me next that you are an emotionally-broken girl with tons of trauma around intimacy, sex, and relationship? Is this meant to be a warning?'

I frowned. 'Are you one of those people?'

'What people?'

'The dickheads on Tinder requesting "good vibes only".' I put down my fork and knife.

'Sorry, it came across wrong. I tried to angle it in a more lighthearted way.'

I took up my cutleries and began eating again.

'Do you really want to know the truth?'

He leaned forward, squinting his icy blue eyes. The colours were so sharp I imagined them being lit up from the inside by blazing fires.

'I never truly believe that I have what it takes . . . for someone to think I'm irreplaceable.'

As the words came out, I regretted them. I should not be appearing pathetic, this was only the first date, and already I was telling him how desperate I was.

'You must think I am desperate.' I could not help adding on to the desperation.

'Oh I assure you, you *are* desperate,' Seth grinned. 'But I get it. 'And I like how open you are about these things. The more you admit it, the less it has power over you.'

'That's an interesting theory.'

'No, I'm serious. I get it. I feel like I do not matter all the time . . . perhaps not in personal relationships. But you know, professional life and all, and I have been pushing so hard.'

I didn't even tell him about my after-graduation plans yet, and what it said about my opinion of my own career potential.

'But it's good to be pushing, that was actually a blessing,' he stretched his arms above his head and yawned. 'You need the insecurity to work harder. Just as yourself, you need feelings to not matter to work towards feeling like you matter for yourself, and that should be enough.'

'That's really wise. I wouldn't expect this from someone like you.'

'Someone *like me?* What did I do wrong?'

It was a lie of course. I knew that he was unusual. I could not even guess at his age. He could be in his late twenties, but his unique appearances made him almost ethereal and ageless.

'Has it been painful? With your skin?' I pointed at his chalk-white hands, green veins popping from underneath.

'I feel very sensitive under the sunlight. I avoid the sun like vampires.'

'We are going out in bright daylight now.'

'It's fine of course, I'm used to it. Perhaps the sensitivity is something that I imagine in my head, based on what I know about my condition.'

'Self-perpetuating belief.'

'Belief is everything. It changes you at a fundamental level. Our minds are way more powerful than we give them credit for.'

'Now you sound like a New Age Preacher.'

We chuckled again and settled into another comfortable silence, finishing the last scraps of our food and the last drops of our drinks.

I felt slightly dizzy and lightheaded, and warm from all the wine. I noticed that every time he frowned, his jaw lines became punctuated, and his eyes became more ablaze. I thought about how bizarre this whole person was.

'You've got really nice hair, and skin,' he observed, as he motioned at the waiters to clear our plates.

'I am getting tanned,' was my response. I realized how much I looked like a tropical girl, with my waves of jet-black hair that touched upon my shoulders, and olive skin that glowed with Zaneta's tanning coconut oils.

After our meals we walked along the beach, carrying our slippers in our hands, our feet pressing firmly one after another on the gravelly sand. The waves lapped gently on our skin. It felt nice. Our fingertips touched several times, and I felt a tiny surge of electric tingles, however we pretended nothing happened.

'It's possible, you know. Happily ever after. I want you to believe that for yourself,' Seth said, covering his eyes with his hand. 'Damn this sun.'

'There is no forever after. Somebody would die at least,' I tried so hard not to mention Covert.

'You know what I mean.'

I thought about how odd it was, that we were akin to two particles colliding together at a specific intersection of time and place. Without my parents, I would not be here, without the mean girls at school, I would not be applying to schools in Singapore to continue my studies. Without Singapore, I would not be at Harvard. Without Harvard, there would be no Zaneta. Without Zaneta, there would be no Covert, or Florida, or Seth. We did not make plans around each other, yet here we were, talking freely as if we had known each other from before, as if we were merely picking up where we left off. We did not even need to tell each other all our background stories, they did not seem to matter much.

I took a deep breath. 'I want to believe.'

Seth squatted down to extract a broken conch shell from the sand and threw it into the water's horizon. It made several bounces before disappearing into the blue.

'Good. Mark my words, this is going to be the start of everything.'

The ringing phone was not the only thing there was. I recalled wrapped, silk-ribboned boxes hidden under his folded shirts in the drawer, which came to my attention as I developed a habit of going through my parents' belongings when they were out and about. I unwrapped some of them, when possible, when the folding were not taped or glued shut, and easily reversible. I uncovered trinkets, little gold jewellery with crushed diamonds and sapphires. Milky-pearl earrings shaped like tear drops. Once I saw a watch, made from sterling silver and carved with intricate patterns, its face dotted with coloured Swarovski crystals. The last thing I unboxed before I moved to Singapore was a bottle of perfume, I thought I saw the *Chanel* logo on it, and a note that

said, '*Cinta, bila saja kau tahu betapa berharganya senyummu di hatiku.*'[1]
It was all notably cringeworthy, but I was more puzzled more
than anything else, for these sweet words were uncharacteristic
of my father's stern and impenetrable comportment, and just
seeing them written boldly in his broken handwriting made me
feel like crying.

Those gifts could not have been for Mother, for they were
all too cheap, and far too sentimental, loaded with meaning and
chosen care.

He showered Mother with gifts often too, he was a generous
man, and he always made a point to let all of us know whenever
he did something nice for her, a celebratory occasion that called
for dinner at a nice restaurant. After the 1998 disaster, things
seemed to have improved for him, he got hold onto a significant
share in his casino bosses' new ventures—online casinos—and
profits were turning in fast and handsome.

I noticed that we started eating out more, going out to faraway
places during school holidays, such as the United States and
Western Europe, in Asian bus tours that made various stops in
fancy dining and shopping outlets. My mother was speaking about
sending us to a boarding school in Hong Kong or Singapore. My
sister seemed worried, but I was listening eagerly, my ears perked
up in full attention.

He got her huge diamond rings and necklaces for safe
keeping—three carats and above. Leather footwear and
handbags and jackets. Once, a loud, red, Lexus, another time a
cruise holiday package to the Caribbeans. The biggest one must
be the keys to a luxury condominium in Singapore, bought in
full under her name. Every single time, Mother smirked with a
stiff smile and said something to play down his offerings. 'Sure,
if only every single minute he spent with the karaoke girls could

---

[1] 'Love, if only you knew how much your smile was worth in my heart'

be redeemed in diamonds,' she said, laughing and shaking her head. And another, 'I wondered if the car could talk and listen to me like a proper life partner.'

Her words were uncalled for, but they were fair regardless. As my father improved in his economic and societal standing, and their marriage matured, Mother started expecting more from him. Gone were the days when she would dutifully soak his feet in hot water and accept the cash to buy the month's groceries without questions. There was so much more to lose now, and more things to be unhappy about.

I thought about this mistress a lot, this 'Cinta' whoever she was. I thought that she must know Father in a lot of ways that we do not. The ways in which he was a lover, a man of his own passions and interests, his quirks and his charms, his likes and dislikes. I thought about this different Father, the one who I never knew, and I felt a pang of jealousy.

I looked through his sock and underwear drawers, and under his bed, and even unlocked his car and rummaged through the glove compartments, looking for more clues, for more tidbits and trinkets, anything at all. I collected hotel name cards, crumpled into empty boxes of cigarettes. A napkin with red lipstick stains on it. I found two stubs of movie tickets to a local romantic comedy film. He would never go to watch something like that with Mother. I kept all these neatly in a locked tin box and carried the keys in my wallet.

When I was fourteen years old, I became fast friends with a boy who lived in my neighbourhood and rode the same school bus with me. His name was Indra, he was a feminine character who was very popular among girls. We gossiped a lot. After one too many hangouts at the food stalls eating grilled satays after school, I told him about my father's mistress.

'Do you think your mom knows about her?'

'I bet she does. She just does not want to stir any drama.'

'We should find out more about her.'

'You think so?'

'Don't you want to?'

'Yes, but . . . How?'

'We just need to follow him, secretly.'

At fourteen, Indra knew how to ride a motorbike and drive a car. Despite his predilection for chatter and gossip, his sentimental heart and his feminine gaits, he was a daring, mischievous boy on his own rights. Both of his parents travelled often for work, and being an only child, Indra had all the time in the world to figure out how to do things on his own. There was a Toyota sedan that was sitting in the garage for him to use, and I could not wrap my head around the idea that he had the means to go anywhere, anytime he wanted.

We hatched a plan. In the evenings after dinner, when Father made a move to his work affairs, Indra would follow him with his sedan and watch him closely until he got back again. I told him that Father was often out the whole night and only came back at dawn, and that Indra could not possibly follow him all the way, but he told me that he did not need much sleep—he was always up all night playing video games anyway, so following my father would be no problem at all.

'Please don't get caught,' I told him. And 'How could I ever repay you?'

'I won't. And you don't have to. I'd love to do it.'

So he did that about three times a week over a period of ten weeks or so, alternating between the days he went. I saw him nodding off in classes, on top of our glossy big algebra textbook. He slipped to the school clinic every other day to complain about punishing headaches and take a nap. Our matron loved him because he often dropped by to feed her sweets and staff gossip.

During this period, he gave me the low-down about Cinta every Friday after school at our grilled satay hangout stalls.

'She lives in a modern, medium-sized house in the upscale neighbourhood in Pluit, by the harbour,' he informed me. 'I saw your father going in there every Tuesday and Wednesday after his business meetings and leaving by the break of dawn.'

'She drives an Audi.' And upon seeing my face, 'A small one, probably second hand. It looked old.'

'Where does she drive to?'

'Well, I followed her a couple of times on the weekends. She goes to the shopping malls in central and south Jakarta. She goes to the salon, to the spa and massage outlets.'

'What does she buy?'

'I'd need a binocular to get the deets, but I supposed I saw nice monochrome shopping bags, perhaps LV and Chanel and the likes. You know, the usual.'

'What else?'

'She frequents the nice cafes in Kemang and other places. She goes to drink often, and I saw her chatting and laughing with many older men . . . And other ladies as well. She went salsa dancing once, and to that club Podium another time.'

'You think my father is not her only patron?'

'Certainly not. He only comes on Tuesdays and Wednesdays. I saw other cars in her driveway on Mondays, Thursdays, and Fridays. She did not seem to welcome any guests on the weekends. Sometimes I saw a few ladies coming in, probably her friends.'

I thought about my mother, who had no friends, who had never been with any other man and had married my father right after high school.

'She could be meeting real boyfriends on the weekends, I'm not sure,' Indra said. 'I saw her going to an upscale condominium at Kebon Jeruk a couple of times now.'

At the ten weeks mark, Indra reported to me that Cinta was traveling overseas. 'She left Sunday afternoon, straight to the airport. She was carrying a posh Tumi's suitcase, and she wore brand clothing from head to toe.' He shrugged. 'I would guess, probably a holiday to Europe? She was wearing a light white coat with fur trimmings on top. It's unlikely she is going to Bali, is my take.'

'You are really good at this,' I pointed out.

Indra waved his hand dismissively. 'Really, don't mention it.' As a final bonus, he showed me a few long-distance snaps he took of her with his polaroid camera. They were blurry and out of focus, but I could see a petite woman, slightly plump and voluptuous, with long wavy black hair that fell all the way to her lower back. She had generous lips and a big wide smile.

Mother rarely smiled. Hers was stiff like a thin line. I thought about her strict dietary regime, her compulsive obsession with keeping calorie count, her midnight carrot and celery sticks for snacks. I thought about countless hours of her faithful Pilates and calisthenic exercises at our home gym. She had the same waist measurement as she did when she was seventeen, and a pair of silicone-filled breasts that she had done in South Korea five years ago.

'I really appreciate what you have done so far,' I told Indra. 'You really need not do so much. You are clearly losing sleep over this.'

Indra patted my shoulder, 'Look, Cassie. If anyone should feel bad about anyone, it should be *me* feeling bad about your shit father.'

That statement took me by surprise, I did not realize that I had not been thinking that way. I was not trying to get to the offending truth, for I had known about it for many years now, I was just trying, in fact, to get closer to him.

I motioned to the waiter to get our bill and insisted on paying everything. 'Shit father gave me enough pocket money,' I said, trying to lighten the mood of everything. Indra was looking at me with concerned eyes. He wrapped his arms around my shoulder and gave me a warm long hug.

All I could think about was how Cinta had such a good life. I never knew that a woman could really have it all.

A couple of months after that, I won a government scholarship to Singapore for my high school. My parents were ecstatic—Singapore was the prime destination for a world class education in Southeast Asia, yet it was still very close to Indonesia that they would still be able to see me often. The scholarship meant that I was smart, and they could now brag about it to their friends and relatives.

I moved countries soon after my junior high graduation with the international school in Tangerang. I packed all my belongings with me into two big suitcases, except for the tin box bearing trinkets from my father's affairs. I gave these to Indra.

'Keep it, please. I'll come and get them back one day.'

I never had the chance to collect them. When I called up Indra's home after my time in the United States, his mother picked up to tell me that in the decade and half that I had been overseas Indra had earned a culinary degree, became a chef, quit his job, and turned into a traveling yoga teacher and tarot reader. It was impossible to pin him down—as he was always on the move. I asked her whether she had seen or known any tin box among his possessions.

'I'm sorry dear, I'm afraid I gave most of them away to charity . . .'

I bid her thankyou and hung up. By then, my father's affair with Cinta had long ended. It was just as well.

Chapter Nine

The Beginning of The Ending

Zaneta called me on my cell. 'Hello. Where are you at? We have been missing you the whole day.'

'I'm outside, with a friend.'

'Like who?' An edge in her voice. 'I didn't know you knew anyone here.'

'It's a kid next door. I just met him yesterday. He's kinda ... cool.'

'Well—I am now out fishing with Covert . . . Over at the Causeway Park . . .' I could almost hear her rolling her eyes. 'I was supposed to have a video chat with Blake thirty minutes ago, but Covert needs to talk when he is waiting to catch the fish . . . And I did not really want to bug you . . . But I really need a little break. I was expecting you to call.'

'I'm sorry. I understand. I'll be there.'

'Are you nearby?'

'Actually I don't know. Let me check.' I opened my map application—it would take around thirty minutes on Seth's motorbike to get there. 'Thirty minutes ETA,' I told her.

'Alright. That's fine.' The phone clicked shut. I looked at Seth. 'I need your help . . . To get to Causeway Park. My friend is there now, and she needs me to come over to help with something.'

'Your sorority sisters? Fishing?' He raised his eyebrows. 'I didn't know if that is a thing that hot college girls would dig.'

'We are the most environmentally-conscious sorority on campus,' I heard myself speak. 'We enjoy all nature activities—it's different. Could I get a lift then?'

'Sure. My pleasure,' He bowed down a little bit. 'I'm here at your service.'

I hopped on the backseat of the motorbike and Seth started the engine. From West Palm Beach, we roared through the highway towards the north. The sun above roasted the insides of my helmet, and the strap was flapping against my chin, but I pressed my chest against Seth's back and wrapped my arms around his waist, and I could feel my heart beat a little faster.

I could not quite pinpoint this feeling I had for Seth, it was not like the bittersweet yearning I felt for my junior high school crush in Indonesia, neither was it the lukewarm fondness I had for the boyfriend in Singapore's boarding school, or the confusing erotic charges I felt around Zaneta, or the throbbing desire for any of my college hookups. This feeling was precious and private. If Zaneta opened me up into new frontiers, being around Seth felt like returning home, to some pristine, intimate parts of me that I thought I had lost forever.

I had this habit of going out of my mind to inspect how I related to others around me. It was not to compare, but merely to observe, and perhaps to take a healthy, protective distance from this subject of affection. I knew my heart beat faster around Seth, yet somehow I felt safe around him. I knew that I still needed to be cautious. Safety was a privilege, and most probably an illusion, as with almost everything else in life.

'Hanging in there?' Seth yelled over his shoulder, from behind his helmet visor.

'I'm having the time of my life!' I yelled back, the strong air pressure hitting my cheeks and sending tears to my eyes. My teeth trembled with the reverberation of the charging motorbike.

I could hear him laugh, and it made me laugh again. It was oddly comfortable, to be laughing like this, on a speeding motorbike. I tightened my grip around him and buried my nose on his leather jacket, like it was the most natural thing in the world to do.

In about exactly thirty minutes Seth pulled over by the pier of the Causeway Park. He helped me get down from my seat. 'Shall I walk you over?'

'No—no, that's fine,' I said, perhaps a little too quickly. Seth frowned a little. 'They are quite exclusive you see . . . this is not like a group of friends—there are rules and codes of conduct.'

'And thank you so very much for the ride,' I added. 'I'll take it from here.'

'Alright,' He put on his helmet, but took it off again. 'I was not going to ask . . . but then I thought, hell you are leaving soon, there is no time to play games. When can I see you next?'

I did not intend to play games, but I was not entirely sure what Zaneta's response might be if I disappeared again this week. 'I don't know,' I said truthfully.

'Aw. Come on here, I said no playing games. Did you not enjoy hanging out with me?'

'Yes, I did. But I seriously don't know.'

'The sorority sisters again?'

'Yes . . .'

He shook his head. 'Well if this goes on, I'd dare to guess that you are actually a kidnapped hostage to a sorority cult, and you have developed some kind of Stockholm Syndrome so you get to go around but you always return to the cult.'

'Ha ha! That's funny. No, seriously I'd love to hang out a few times with you before I leave. Of course, are you kidding me? We get along so well! But I can't promise yet . . . I'd know by tonight I suppose.'

'Alright then, I'd wait for you tomorrow . . .? Perhaps 2 p.m., same place? If you don't show up in thirty minutes . . . I'll take it that you're not available . . .'

'Can't we just exchange numbers like normal people? I'll text you.'

'Right. There's that.'

I saved his number in my phone and gave him a smile that I thought looked promising. His hand reached out and touched my cheek. I felt goosebumps on my skin, I knew what he was going to do next. I saw him lean forward and I braced myself—our lips touched. His tongue brushed on my lower lip before he sucked it gently. I held my breath the entire time.

There was nothing left to be said, for the last time Seth put on his helmet and drove back to where we came from. I watched his bike turn into the highway and disappeared among a flow of cars.

I turned around and walked towards the pier, looking for Zaneta and Covert. They were standing by the edge, looking at his fishing pole, bobbing on the clear water. 'There you are,' Zaneta looked at me, covering her eyes with her hand.

'There you are,' Covert parroted. He cocked his head to the left. 'Look at what I've got over there . . . some fresh tunas!'

I looked at a pile of three big fish flailing in a bucket on the dock next to him. 'How fun.'

'Who's your friend? Tell us about him!' Zaneta plonked herself on a folding chair set up by the pier. 'Were you on a date, or what?'

I was not sure how to answer, or whether there would be a perceived conflict of interest, but my instinct was to deny. 'No—he was just like . . . my age . . . you know? So we vibed on certain things.'

'Well, is he paying you to hang out with him?' the edge in her voice again, sharp and accusatory.

'Alright princess, don't be like that,' Covert chuckled. 'I don't mind really.'

'Well, we don't want anyone to take advantage of you, Pumpkin. Cassie is my dear friend and I love her with all my heart, but she needs to know that a job is a job, and she needs to be clear that she's on duty at the moment.'

'You have made that absolutely clear.' I said, 'I'll stick around.'

'Good.' Zaneta gave me a look. It was a side of her I had never seen before, it was as if she had turned into a different person— meaner and sharper. She must have felt threatened somewhat, perhaps I could ruin the whole thing for us, by falling in love. *But how about Blake.*

'Alright, I have a call to make now, if you'd excuse me . . .' She reached out and squeezed my left shoulder, took out her phone and walked away.

'Well, do you want to try fishing? What do you think, eh?'

Blake had been Zaneta's primary boyfriend ever since I met her. I was not sure how they met, I always thought that she was too good for him. Blake was tall and lanky, and faded. His colouring looked like washed up water colours. He always had glasses on, sporadic stubble on his chin, a skinny face and even a skinnier nose. His eyes though, were beautiful. They were golden brown, like two oval amber stones, shaded under curly thick lashes. He was pursuing a PhD in History for as long as I remembered, his subject focus was Israel–Palestinian war.

'That is a very important undertaking,' was what I told him when we first met. 'I'm sure you are very proud of yourself.'

'Well as you can see, I'm so committed to it, in fact I'm dating an Israelian,' he pushed his glasses up and smiled at me. We were sitting in their flat's living room, filled with neon-coloured furniture and an inflatable unicorn. The only thing that was his seemed to be a large parchment map of the middle east covering the whole side of a wall.

'So you are on the Jewish side then?'

'This is a tricky question, one that is fraught with problematic assumptions that this is a war between the Jewish and the Arabs ...'

'Oh, please don't let him start,' Zaneta uncorked a bottle of wine and started pouring into our glasses. 'We are both solidly on the side of peace. Peace does not cost us anything, and I was not sure what these guys have been doing, really ...' She shrugged her shoulders and drained her glass.

I really was not sure what brought them together.

'Hey I am doing my part, alright,' Zaneta laughed and messed up my hair a little bit. 'I am manifesting a brighter future for all of us, every day. Remember? Positive mind ... Come on?'

It was an invitation to repeat after her.

'Positive mind emits a positive wavelength that bends reality for the highest good of everyone,' Blake and I said in a familiar chorus.

'Every. Single. Thought. Counts,' she giggled and tapped on the tip of Blake's nose.

There was something impenetrable about Blake—his eyes glazed behind his glasses, as if unseeing. I could not guess what he was thinking most of the time. He talked in a reasoned, measured voice, always calm, always soothing. He enjoyed dishing neutral historical facts, and almost always agreed to anything. For a scholar, he did not seem to have any opinion on his own.

He must be very grounding for all of her electricity—however I wondered if they even had sex at all. Zaneta kept telling me that he had bouts of depression and surely that must translate to a lack of sex drive. They have an open relationship—Zaneta was always active with her polyamorous communities—cuddle buddies and group sex. I knew she had a few regular lovers that come and go. They were almost always muscular with chiselled faces. I also knew that there was a black girl who kept hanging around, without ever introducing herself to me. She had luscious dark skin like chocolate and a faint smell of spices and sex. I thought I heard them moaning in the bedroom one day, as I was camping in the living room, doing my problem sets next to Blake typing furiously on his computer. As for me, I was never sure how I was configured exactly in Zaneta's life.

I always thought that my position in her constellation of lovers and admirers was never secure, that at any moment she would turn around and leave me cold and hanging—just like all the other lovers in my life.

Secretly I believed that nobody had ever really seen me and therefore they would not remember anything. I was readily forgotten after I was introduced, I was readily abandoned after I was befriended, dated, and cared for. This deep-seated belief made me jolt with delightful surprise every time I received a text message from her, asking me to join her latest antics and escapades. Somehow, she remembered, even if she did not show it most times, and I noticed that by that spring break of my senior year, I had become one of Zaneta's closest confidantes in all of her years living in Cambridge.

The fishing rod was vibrating suddenly. Covert leaned back and yanked the whole thing out of the water with a great force. 'Check out this beauty,' a fat, glistening red snapper flailed desperately at the end of the hook, its mouth opening and closing steadily.

'Are you going to eat that?'

'Yeah sure, why not,' He threw the snapper on top of the other three. 'I think I have outdone myself for the day . . . I would probably give two of these to the Warrens and we can feast on the remaining two.'

'That sounds good.'

I did not feel like I contributed a lot in keeping him entertained, and I wondered if there was really a need for me to stand by here. Zaneta set the rules, and it seemed like it was in the best interest of everyone that someone was always present at his side. Perhaps she was concerned that he might take off his life a little bit too early, or at all. Perhaps she planned on saving him after all.

Covert went to a food truck nearby to get two bottles of cold beer and passed one to me. We sat side by side on the folding chairs and watched the sunset, a gigantic orange orb bleeding on the horizon.

'You are a quiet girl,' Covert offered his observation.

'People have said that about me,' I said. 'I talk sometimes. It's a vibe thing.'

'Well, listen here. It is Princess's idea that she needed a substitute, not mine.'

'So you don't want me to be here?' I was almost surprised.

'No, no, it's not that at all. I just don't want you to think that I have this idea of having a harem or a creep . . . You know?'

'You are not exactly vanilla either. I don't know anyone else who's digging breast milk.'

'Yeah . . . you're right.' Covert chuckled, and I did too. It was the first time ever we had laughed together.

'That was . . . *creepy*.' I said, emboldened by our burgeoning sense of familiarity.

'I had only one sex partner in my life . . . Until two years ago. One! I am seventy-six! Would you blame a poor loyal chap like me who's rushing to make up for lost time?'

'Sure, that makes sense. What was the weirdest thing you had ever done?'

He looked down at his hands. 'I don't know . . . I went to Japan when I first started exploring. And it was quite wild. I bought used underwear from a vending machine and smelled it during foreplay . . .'

'Say no more,' I held up my hand.

He chuckled again. 'Well in Thailand, I had sex with a ladyboy . . .'

'Man, you are really going places!' I offered my beer bottle for a cheer, and he toasted me gleefully. We gulped down the remaining beer that we had. 'Look at you! And you were . . . seventy-four back then, and all alone, and trying all these things. I think it must have taken a lot of courage.'

'I wasn't alone though,' Covert corrected. 'Zaneta was always there, of course. She pushed my limits, always. I wouldn't even have dreamt to realize any of these fetishes without her. And she gave me new inspiration too. And . . . the more I got into it . . . The more it all became natural for me. Suddenly a whole new world opened, and there was no turning back.'

Somehow my brain felt puzzled, like something was not clicking right. I was certain that there was a missing piece somewhere, it felt like a phantom itch that I could not quite identify. Then it hit me. I had an image playing of Zaneta in the living room, opening her suitcase and distributing interesting wasabi snacks and pieces of technology that you would not find in the United States, such as a torch light that doubled as a motorized small fan. She had just got back from Japan. She told me that she went there with the extension school's summer program. 'Here, it's for you!' She tossed me a Doraemon soft toy with a flourish. 'I'm not sure what that is, but the guy told me this is a famous cartoon character.'

'It is a cat robot from the future,' I explained. 'It has this magic pocket with all sorts of high-tech inventions.'

I remembered that scene in the living room vividly—because I still had the Doraemon back in my college dorm room. That was exactly three summers ago, months before Zaneta's graduation.

'I thought . . . I thought Zaneta started seeing you after she finished her degree . . . Isn't it?'

'Huh?' Covert cocked his head to one side. 'I don't understand.'

'Yeah, she graduated two years ago . . . This is the third year, the final year that you are living your life like there is no tomorrow, the final year before you are going to take your life, the final year that you'd need extra support, hence why I am brought here.'

Covert attempted a smile, but it came across like an uncanny grin, the corner of his lips raised to uncover two rows of big yellow teeth.

'When did Margaret pass?'

'I'm not sure I'm following what you are trying to get at.'

'What I am trying to get at is . . . why did you visit Japan with Zaneta three years ago, a year before the passing of your wife, a year before you were supposed to start a sugar dating arrangement with her? The story did not add up!'

Covert sighed. 'What do you want me to say? She was dying, Cassie, she was on a life support system, catatonic in our bedroom.'

'So you were cheating on her?' My voice trembled with a mixture of emotions that came from nowhere.

He looked down on his stacks of fishes. They were still opening and closing their mouths and trembled ever so slightly. 'I'm not entirely proud of myself . . .'

I did not know why it mattered so much, as what he said, she was already dying—but I felt prickly, almost betrayed. Maybe it's really not about him cheating, maybe it's really about my mother, and feeling like I am somewhat complicit in helping out a man cheating on the memory of his late wife. Maybe it was my own morality that was at stake, or what I perceived as my moral values. It was almost romantic and heroic to help a man reunite again with the love of his life, but the premise of the suicide pact was hanging so precariously on a delicate thread separating between what was right and what was wrong, and so any slight imperfection to this forever-after true love affair threatened to snap it apart.

Or maybe I just wanted to make sure that his intention was truthful to what he declared.

'You really should make good of your promise to her,' I heard myself saying.

'Oh yes I will. Yes I will,' Covert looked at me with a deep frown. 'I'm offended that you would even question it. What else do you think I am doing now, at this very moment?'

I shrugged, feeling suddenly exhausted.

We were both relieved by Zaneta coming back from her calls. She was radiant and satisfied. 'Blake sent his love to the both of you,' she said. 'He is defending his dissertation these days . . . It's very difficult for him. He needs to talk to me a lot . . .' For as long as I could remember, it had always been 'very difficult' for Blake, he seemed to choose to live on a difficult plane of reality.

'It's alright Princess, I don't mind. I know that you've got a heart of gold, and I know that you need to take care of people that you love . . .' Covert gave her a long hug. They looked at each other for some time, and I saw gentleness in her eyes. Right then, I realized that her feelings for him were, in fact, *genuine*. My stomach felt heavy like I just swallowed rocks.

* * *

'Cassie pointed out to me, today, that we have to start coming up with a concrete plan.'

We were back in the living room at the penthouse, sipping pink fruit cocktails and eating cucumber sandwiches that Zaneta made for us—her idea of a good evening snack. She chewed on her sandwich thoughtfully, her brow furrowed like she was confused. 'It is still a year away, what plan are you talking about?'

'Oh, but yes, we need to start the discussion, you know, to keep the motivation alive and well, to oil the engine before we start.'

'Cassie told you *that*?'

I felt exposed, like I was perhaps doing something wrong. Increasingly I felt like I could not do anything right and that I had to walk on eggshells around Zaneta, and I hated the feeling. It was not supposed to be like this. It was as if she had turned into a different person, someone that I did not fall in love with.

'Yes, that was part of the job description, isn't it? Are you going to find anything else that is wrong with *that*?' I reacted, harsher than I intended.

Her jaws relaxed and her eyes grew bigger. She was instantly magnetic again. 'Sweetie, I am not your enemy. Remember that. There's nothing wrong with anything. I, for one, studied positive psychology and I think overplanning and over worrying for something so far ahead is completely unnecessary. It'll make us anxious.'

Covert and I looked at each other, as if we were just being scolded by our mother.

'I think a better focus for us now is to make sure that the following year will be unforgettable and memorable for all of us, a year filled with joy, warmth, intimacy, and growth . . . isn't that right?'

I could not wrap my head around this. I wondered how she processed the world around her and made her judgement. She sounded like a saccharine fairy godmother stock character in cheap soap operas, the ones peddling 'love, live, and joy', constantly smiling, constantly encouraging, constantly saying that everything is going to be alright, even when buildings were burning down to ashes all around her.

I felt like screaming and shaking her body. *But he's going to die! What are you talking about? He is going to die and we need to do the work to make sure everything is going to be alright!*

Zaneta looked like she could read my mind. She smiled and finished the last drop of her cocktail, and with a voice that struck me as utterly cold she said, 'Covert dear, now would you give us a minute? I need to talk to Cassie in private.'

'Oh dear, I hope that I did not cause any trouble. Listen Princess, I think Cassie is right. We need to think of options, starting now.' He began pacing up and down the room. 'It is not going to be that easy, you know. Which method are we going to use? How are we going to make it look like a solo suicide? How to make sure that I won't implicate the both of you? How can I make good on my promise, of passing my inheritance, without drawing unnecessary attention from the authorities? Come on Princess, it is still a year away but I want the best outcome for all of us.'

'What about setting up a trust?' I offered. 'Like a structure in BVI or in Dubai or Switzerland, with complete anonymity and protection of the beneficiaries of that trust. I think that could work, couldn't it? And we could then . . . take it out slowly . . . Maybe over the years . . . Lay low for a little bit.'

Covert looked at me, a little bit impressed. 'How would you know about this? I think that's exactly it . . . That was what I was thinking. . . My brother is a corporate lawyer . . . But I don't think it is a good idea to enroll his help. He'd have questions, and by the way, he would certainly have questions on my assets and properties once my death would be announced.'

I took a course on international ethics and regulations around white-collar crimes once—it was offered jointly with the Harvard Law School.

'As I said, you could set aside something liquid now, that would pay us for the few years after your suicide, and keep the rest in the trust. Write your brother a letter, saying that you have made your will and asking him to respect that. Perhaps give him a little bit of money as well to keep him satisfied . . .'

'That bastard. He does not deserve even a single penny from me!' Covert snorted. 'He had stopped speaking to me ever since our Ma passed away. He was always jealous of my successes, because he thought he was smarter . . .'

'Carbon monoxide poisoning still seems to be one of the best options in my opinion,' I ventured again. 'Earlier on this year there was this homicide case in Indonesia, a girl poisoning her girlfriend by putting some cyanide in her coffee. That was speedy and instantaneous.'

'Ah, interesting.' Covert tapped his chin with his fingers. 'Is that painful?'

'If hydrogen cyanide is inhaled it can cause a coma with seizures, apnea, and cardiac arrest, with death following in a matter of seconds,' I read out loud from my phone, quoting Wikipedia.

'We definitely should bookmark that.'

'Owh, what if Zaneta and I take off to a separate location for a holiday—one week before the day of your suicide?' I could not stop myself, I was bursting with ideas, they all came very naturally. 'So when the police come to investigate, there will be records of us checking into a hotel away from the location. Oh, and . . . and . . .! You should also write a general farewell letter to the world, announcing your reunification with Margaret. Your motivation must be as clear as daylight for everyone to see.'

Covert nodded, massaging his temple. 'I might need some moral support though . . . What if I need you girls to administer the poison?'

I was about to answer but fell silent again. I imagined standing by his bedside, tilting a cup of cyanide-laced milk towards his open mouth. His head cradled in my arm, tears streaming down his papery skin.

The room grew quiet. It was pitch black outside now, a rare moonless night. The sea breeze blew gently into the room. I hugged my elbow tightly, feeling cold so suddenly.

'Alright, again, my dears . . . May I have a moment with Cassie please?' Zaneta repeated.

Covert sank back on the sofa, breathing deeply. His whole face slackened, and suddenly he looked as if he had grown ten years older. 'Sure, sure . . . Actually . . . I think I can make use of some rest now . . .'

He stood up and shuffled slowly into his room. His bedroom door clicked shut gently. It was just me and Zaneta now and she was not looking pleased. 'What was that all about?'

'What about it?'

'Did you not hear what I said—that we must focus on love and positivity?'

'Did you not hear what he said? What if he needs us to actually pull the plug—can we please settle first on who is going to do it?'

'I can't believe we are having this conversation, this is so morbid!' She made a little frustrated yelp, and shook her Shirley Temple curls furiously.

'You are acting like a child right now! You *came to me* with this proposal—what are you expecting, really?'

She was breathing very hard, her cheeks flushed, her green eyes looked like two flaming slits. 'If you have your way, you'd prefer him dead at the end of this very spring break, wouldn't you?'

Her words were ice cold, and I heard my heartbeat louder in my ears.

'Wouldn't you? You'd rather have him kill himself now, and pass you his fortunes now, so that you could get away without even sleeping with him once, wouldn't you? So that you could ride off to the sunset with your new boyfriend on a white horse, wouldn't you?'

'*Wouldn't you??*' Her voice rose an octave higher. 'I can't believe this! You have been very insistent on having this conversation, you are not even ashamed at the very least about it...'

I stayed very quiet still.

'What are you made of, really? Are you really *that* cruel?'

'Look, Zaneta. It was *his* idea, and *your* idea . . . You brought me here . . .'

'I brought you here to give him joy and pleasure, I brought you here so that the poor grieving man would have company 24/7 by his side. I brought you here to satisfy his sexual cravings, true to his last wish on earth. I did not bring you here to try to manipulate the whole situation to your own selfish advantage!'

'You are twisting everything, completely, Zane. Please calm down. I am not trying to manipulate anyone for selfish reasons . . .'

She walked towards me and took my chin in-between her thumb and forefinger. Her bubblegum-coloured nails dug into my skin. 'Prove it, then. Prove it. Have sex with him tonight. He has been very patient with you.'

I knew that there was no way I could get away this time round. The whole situation had spiralled out of my hands.

'You mean like, right now?'

'If you want me to be serious about this arrangement, if you want to start planning everything in detail, I need to know that you would pull your weight for one whole year,' she spoke now in a very low tone. 'It's ten million worth of cash, stocks and properties for *you*, Cas. You will never have to work a single day again for the rest of your life. You can do whatever you like, be wherever you like. Your life will be completely *yours*.'

I blinked calmly. What happened next felt dissociative, as if I hovered above my body and watched myself walk slowly towards Covert's room. Zaneta was close on my heels. She turned the doorknob for me and switched on the light.

'Hey Covert? Cassie is ready tonight.'

He was sitting on his bed, only in his polka dot boxers, his chest naked, flaunting curly silver hair. His skin sagged on his long bones—I never noticed how his legs were skinny like two chicken legs, supporting a pot belly on top.

'Oh, really? I was not expecting that.'

'What do you think, are you in the mood tonight, dear?' Her voice went back to her normal state—light and jingly with ever the slightest rasp.

His spectacles reflected the harsh light from the lamp above. I could not see his eyes. 'What question is that, Princess? I am always in the mood, always,' he smacked his lips.

I was wearing a flowery summer dress with a zipper up my back. I stood there, waiting for cues. Zaneta went behind my back and unzipped my dress, it fell down my bare shoulders and piled up on the floors. I wore a plain white bra with lace flowers sewn on top of it, and plain white underwear. I lowered my eyes, I could not look at them.

Covert stood up from the bed and approached me, his breath fogged up his glasses. He touched my arm, traced his finger to my neck and my chin. 'What turns you on? Tell me what turns you on?'

His boxers were yellow with red polka dots. His bare skin moved in tandem with his breathing, looking sallow against my olive skin. I did not feel that I could move or do anything at all— my limbs were heavy with a sense of depression so deep it was tranquilizing. It was interesting, that I felt like I did not have a choice, that I could not possibly have a say in this.

He started kissing the top of my shoulder, and down to the top of my chest—his toothbrush moustache felt bristly and offensive, but I did not know what to do about it.

'Could we play with a blindfold, this time around?' Finally I found my voice before his lips moved to approach mine.

He looked at me momentarily, his eyebrows lifted. 'Well, well, well, that *is* fun . . . There you go . . . I knew you had it in you . . .'

I was surprised that he did not immediately pick up why I suggested a blindfold—perhaps he was that delusional, or perhaps he was pretending to ignore the obvious, pretending and ignoring seemed to be a behavior positively rewarded in this household.

Zaneta went to the bedside drawer and pulled out a long silk ribbon. She came back and made a loop with it round my eyes. Her breath smelled like peppermint sage and it made the hair on my neck stand up. After two rounds, she secured the silk ribbon in a tight knot behind my head—everything became pitch black. I felt her cold fingers pop the clasp of my bra and it fell off to the floor. She pulled at my nipples playfully and bit my earlobe, and with her other fingers she rubbed at the bottom of my underwear. 'You are getting wet,' it was almost like a command.

She pushed me on top of the bed, I was kneeling on all fours, completely in pitch darkness. She was right, I was wet, out of my control, despite Covert, despite everything else. She leaned forward and whispered very softly in my ear: 'Don't worry sweetie. It'll get better with time, I promise.'

She moved away, and I heard a condom plastic wrapper being torn, and some shuffling noises. I could feel Covert now, coming in swiftly. At that precise moment my mind went blank. I felt like nothing, and it was such a relief. I was not my body and my body was not mine. It was simply a vessel, a facilitator, a useful aid. Who I was at the core, I was Cassandra, and I was ethereal. I was above the rest, I was above the world of the flesh.

What came next was a childhood memory that I had forgotten, of me, Mother and my sister, going to a famous American fried chicken restaurant in a family-friendly shopping mall we frequented often, all in good spirits and good laughter. Mother took us to the fried chicken restaurant on the days that report cards were given out at the end of each school semester. She usually banished junk food, but she would award us a trip there for good grades, and for we always had good grades, the fried chicken trip became a given.

Mother was always in a good mood during these trips— perhaps getting our glittering report cards served as a hallmark that something was going well with her life's work. She always ordered chicken breast pieces covered in crumbly crispy skin— as the breast was a healthier choice—with french fries and a mountain of rice. We had packets and packets of chili sauce poured out at the side. It was customary and more satisfying to eat with our hands somehow: we would take a pinch of rice, a piece of chicken, a piece of fries, dipped in chili, crumpled everything into a ball and put it in our mouths. This combination tasted heavenly, and we licked our fingers with big smiles on our faces.

'If only I could feed you girls like this every day,' Mother said.

'Why not?' I asked, chili sauce smeared all over my cheeks.

'Yeah it's very cheap. But it's also unhealthy . . . bad nutrition.'

'I'd like to eat like this every day,' my sister echoed. Her eyes were cheerful behind her pink-rimmed glasses. 'Well if only I could,' Mother patted our heads. 'If only I could then it won't be too expensive to raise the two of you, little devils.'

We giggled.

'Remember girls,' she told us. 'Try to make your own money, as best as you can. Make your own money, if you know how to do it, make your own money. That's the key to your freedom.'

My sister and I nodded absent-mindedly. The fried chicken restaurant was our happy place, and we would eat there every day if we had the choice.

Chapter Ten

The Attic

I remembered a philosophy and ethics class I took as an elective once, somewhere around Junior year. We discussed Hume and Durkheim, Kant and Bentham, Plato and Aristotle. The course had a big section on the ethics of suicide—it was something that I found sufficiently interesting, yet unrelatable to anything that I had experienced or might ever experience in my lifetime. I approached the whole subject as a curious thought exercise.

It was the year that I started getting my footing at Harvard, and felt like I really belonged. I started getting leadership positions in all my clubs. I was getting the drill of the academic load and my GPA improved over time. I had had a few prestigious internships under my belt in the past summers and winters, and felt slightly less anxious about graduation. It was far ahead enough to worry me significantly, and since the job search season had not officially begun, I could at least stay calm in the knowledge that I had done everything I could to maximize my post-graduation employment chances.

That semester, I had streaks of turquoise highlights in my hair and a belly piercing that gave me a newfound halo of coolness. I was dressing better, I built proficiency in dancing and acquired useful knowledge on how to navigate the space around me gracefully. I was not paying much attention to classes—I had mostly only electives left and I did not plan to do any dissertation. Everything was poised to be smooth sailing and easy.

'This class is *soo* dark,' Beverly whispered to me from her chair. She took some time off school and now we were both junior roommates. We had built close friendship from our time together in the theater club.

'A lot of philosophers seemed to think, that suicide was a rightful individual act,' the Professor looked around the semi circular lecture hall with tiers of seats forming a Greek theatre set up. There was a green chalkboard and a podium. The professor was an older white man, tall and balding. Sometimes I paused and everything still seemed momentarily surreal, that I would be sitting here in an American college that I had watched so often in Hollywood movies on the TV screen back home.

The professor went on, 'Beauchamp described the principle of autonomy as asserting "an obligation to respect the decision-making capacities of autonomous persons by not limiting their liberty to affect their choices".'

Meanwhile, David Hume defended a position first put forward by classical Greek scholars that suicide was an honourable act. Hume's argument was based on an appeal to autonomy and utility. In a discussion of several situations in which suicide might be considered, Hume concluded that in some cases it would be in the interests of the individual, their family and society.

'Can anyone give me an example of justified, utility-based suicide?'

A few hands shot up. 'Prisoners of war?' someone was saying.

'Chronically-ill patients?' another quipped.

'Severely disabled people?'

I didn't really bother raising my hand in big lecture-style classes, the professor would not be able to remember and notice everyone, and participation points would be given in the smaller section classes given by teaching assistants.

'A murderer who wants to right his or her wrong?'

'Someone trapped in extreme poverty?'

'Someone trapped in illegal trafficking?'

'Incurable drug addicts?'

The list went on and on. I did not think that there were so many people on earth who deserved to die.

'Yes, if you think about it, our lives should lie in our hands, isn't that right? Especially as modern nations become increasingly secular. Why would the state have any say on what we want to do with our lives?

And what about assisted suicide? What do you guys think about it?'

'That is different,' somebody shouted from the back, without being asked to speak. I saw the same kid from the sex and desire class last year, wearing a backward baseball cap. He seemed to have grown up. He was bigger, more muscular, and there were stubbles on his chin. He must find this topic more interesting than the penis envy.

'Different how?' The professor smiled encouragingly.

'That just ... does not feel right,' he scratched his head. 'Man, that is twisted.'

'Why is that so? If we generally agree that suicide should be a rightful decision to everyone, why is assisting one criminal?'

'It's like ... yes ... it should be your own decision to die by suicide ... But it does not mean that it is a *nice* decision, and that society should encourage it ... And it just feels wrong if someone is doing it for you ... It's almost like ... A murder.'

The boy was exceptionally ineloquent for a Harvard student. I thought that he must have gotten in through an athletic scholarship.

'Alright, but what about someone who *really* wants to die, but he is incapable of killing himself. What about a brain-dead patient in a vegetative state?'

A girl with a short bob raised her hand, 'That is legal in Switzerland.'

'Alright, so where is the line of ethics to consider here?'

I learnt that there was an exceptionally high prevalence of mental illness among individuals who committed suicide, up to ninety-three per cent in fact, according to one research. It had been suggested that for some, a suicide attempt was a person's high-risk strategy for altering their situation—a 'cry for help' so to speak. The intention was not death but another end, perhaps attention, reconciliation or revenge.

'Many suicide attempts involve ambivalence, they might alternate between wanting to live and wanting to die,' said the Professor. 'In such cases, what is a more ethical thing to do, encouraging the person to continue living, or taking his life?'

'Continue living,' a few voices spoke in unison. Nobody dared to say the latter.

'Aha—so those of you who spoke . . . are supporting the principle of respect for life? Or perhaps the moral duty of that said individual for others, to keep on living?'

His voice grew softer and softer within my field of hearing. I saw his lips opened and closed, but I was checking out. I did not have any answer to any of the questions being posed. It was all too hard.

The next morning, I opened my eyes and stared at the ceiling. The string to the attic glinted in the sunlight, swaying ever so slightly. Covert was snoring gently beside me, his legs splayed liberally across the bed.

I thought about last night. I thought about how I felt this morning. At surface level, it was not that much of a difference. The chain of events was blurry, I could not recall any specific sensation or emotion that was vivid enough to leave any impression.

Instead, I thought about David, how I would sleep snuggling against his chest every day that we spent together. How he would kiss my forehead and stroke my hair. We spent more time cuddling than having sex in fact, and now, looking back, I understood that our fondness for each other was instantaneous and genuine.

I thought about snuggling against Covert's chest, but I could not even imagine it. Had I irreversibly sacrificed something of myself, a piece of me that I could never claim back? Had I woken up a changed young woman?

'Hello sweetheart,' Covert opened his eyes. I jumped off the bed, almost in a knee-jerk moment. In that instance I knew that it would never get better.

'I need to find Zaneta,' I declared. 'This is Wednesday . . . two more days before I have to return to campus.'

'And? Please relax, enjoy yourself a little bit.'

'We needed to discuss some stuff—logistics and such . . .' I picked up my sundress from the floor and slipped it over my head hastily. I pulled my hair up into a ponytail. Covert was eyeing my every move, his moustache twitched.

'Did you enjoy yourself last night?'

I gave him a weak smile. I could not even bring myself to lie or tell him the truth—that my brain seemed to have completely blocked the memory overnight. I threw my phone and wallet into a handbag and put on my sneakers. 'I'll be back.'

With that I charged out of the room and pressed the button to call the elevator of the penthouse.

I wondered how long more he would tolerate me. Certain shades of guilt creeped up and constricted my chest, then my throat. I brushed them aside.

My hands trembled as I exited the condominium out to the bright sunlight outside. My phone showed the time—it was only half past ten in the morning. I did not know where to go or what to do. I reckoned Zaneta was still sleeping in her room, but I did not feel like it made any sense at the moment to go to her.

I took out my phone, pressed a string of numbers and held it against my ear. I waited.

'Hello?' A cool voice croaked in my ear. 'Hello—Seth?'

'Cassie?'

'Yes—urm listen, are you still down to hangout today?'

'Yeah sure. When?'

'Like, right now?'

There was a little bit of silence. 'Is everything alright?'

'Sure, why would anything not be alright?'

'Well, it just seems so sudden . . . And so early . . .'

'It's almost eleven. And I'm spontaneous. And I know you work on your own schedule.'

He chuckled. 'In other words, you think that I will be so free to accompany you at any time of the day.'

'Aren't you?'

'For you, sure. Anything.'

I could feel myself holding a smile. 'There seems to be a little bit of a heatwave today, I think we should just stay indoors.'

'You mean . . . like Netflix and chill?'

'Sure thing.'

'I can order pizza for lunch.'

'Sounds good.'

'Where are you at? I'll pick you up now.'

I gave him Covert's condominium address and he told me he would be here in fifteen minutes.

I was not sure why I contacted Seth—he obviously wanted something I might not be in the best mental space to give. I had nowhere else to go, there was only Zaneta, Bonnie, and Ali, besides Covert. I considered how I should just buy a flight ticket back to Boston tonight.

Seth came to pick me up in under ten minutes. As I hopped onto his bike, a sense of lightness rose in my chest. He had this effect on me. Everything I worried about vanished immediately, my previous stream of thoughts felt inconsequential in the intensity of his presence.

'All good?'

I nodded and gave him a tight hug. I was so grateful to have him right now.

The bike roared along the main road, making a circuitous route towards the south. Seth made a turn into a housing complex with palatial mansions lined along both sides of the street. I saw a variety of intriguing designs—from houses with elaborate Victorian carving facades to those with metal and steel architecture that looked like spaceships.

I felt a sense of almost relief as he pulled over next to a palatable stone-and-wood-and-glass bungalow, designed like a rather high-end cabin in the woods. It was pleasant to look at. 'Great design,' I complimented.

'Yeah, it's pretty new too,' He helped me off the bike. 'We had a massive renovation a couple years back.'

'Your parents must be doing very well.'

He grinned. 'What should I say—they are successful entrepreneurs. I'll outdo them of course . . . In this lifetime. I have it in me, it's genetic.'

'Will I get to see them?'

'Not today, they are actually in DC at the moment, meeting a business partner. Soon though,' He added with a wink. 'If you come back often enough.'

The interior of the house was all polished marbles and wood and glass. Everything was made in earthy colour tones like black, white, gray, and brown. There was a gated brick fireplace occupying a big section in the living room facing opposite an array of leather sofas. A giant plasma TV hung on the walls above the fireplace.

We sat side by side on the sofa. Seth pulled out his phone and ordered a box of cheese and pepperoni pizza online. He turned on the TV and asked me what I would like to watch. I thought that all of it was tediously perfunctory.

'I don't know, maybe something funny?'

'What is funny for you?'

'Is that a test?'

We settled on *Brooklyn Nine-Nine* and watched Captain Holt embark on a poker—face staring challenge with Detective Rosa Diaz. 'They are great. My favourite characters,' Seth pointed at the screen.

'Rosa is my favourite character,' I agreed. 'She's the coolest.'

Seth placed his left hand on my knee, eyes still glued to the screen. I looked at that hand long enough until he looked at it as well, it was hanging there awkwardly like a dead weight. We lifted our eyes and locked gazes and burst out laughing.

'Well, *that was smooth*,' I said. He blushed a little bit, I never thought I could make him blush.

I leaned over and kissed him gently on the lips. He told me it was nice, pulled my head closer and kissed me longer. His other hand slipped underneath my shirt and my bra. My breath became hurried, my cheeks flushed with desire, but it was different than anything I had experienced before. My longing for him was tender, almost painful, and wherever he touched me prickled with electricity. I was afraid I would come just by him touching my breasts like that.

'Wait stop,' I said, breathless, pushing him off me. 'Stop for a minute.'

He crouched at the edge of the sofa, suddenly cool, watching me with a steady gaze.

'I'm sorry . . . I don't think I can . . . No . . . not today.'

'I can wait, no pressure.' He touched my cheek. 'We've got all the time in the world.'

'No, you don't know . . . I'm not . . . I'm not going to be *good* for you.'

His eyes turned into slits, he jumped off in one swift motion and went away to get us glasses of water. I thought he was going to laugh at what I said, but he did not. He was waiting.

I thought about Covert last night, breathing on my neck, his chest pressed against my back.

'I have someone else,' I said. 'Maybe for another year.'

He was drinking his water, and now he burst out laughing. 'You've got a boyfriend . . . just for another year?'

'Sort of.'

'What is this—a contract boyfriend? An arranged marriage? Are you married . . . For a green card?'

I could not help laughing too. 'Yes, you could say that . . .' I shook my head. 'Actually, fuck, that's about right.'

'I would *marry you*,' he said, without blinking.

'I'm touched by your heartfelt proposal,' I said. 'But my arrangement is . . . a little bit more complicated than that.'

'Okay, are you pregnant?'

'No! Of course not!'

'Are you in love with him?'

'No . . . not him. But I'm in love with someone else. I think.'

'You are not here for your sorority sisters' trip, aren't you?'

I shook my head. 'Wasn't that obvious?'

He waited again.

'I did not tell you—the full truth . . . But I'm here with my girlfriend . . . Well not a romantic one, but not exactly a platonic one either. I'm not sure what we are actually . . . And she has, she has this sugar daddy who is recruiting for a second sugar baby to accompany him for one more year. So we can take turns . . . You know? My girlfriend has a primary boyfriend she needs to attend to regularly.'

As I uttered the story I watched Seth closely, but he seemed to remain calm and unaffected. 'Is there a *recruiting* process for sugar babies?' was his only response.

'I thought it was . . . It was interesting, you know. And it's just one year . . . And the payout will be more than I would probably be able to make in this lifetime.' I could not help it, I was justifying myself.

'Are you saying . . .'

'The old man wants to die, alright. He's seventy-six and he wants to die. In a year's time. And he's going to put us in his will and pass us millions. Ten for me, he promised ten million in cash and other assets.'

I heard myself recount the story and it sounded perfectly sound and reasonable to me.

Seth remained quiet so I continued, 'We are going to help him die. That's the plan. We have not really thought about it in detail, but we are going to help him, no matter what. If he needs help, we are going to help him . . .'

'You are going to make sure that the old man takes his own life? For ten million?'

I saw that his blue eyes were of different colours now—they were darker, almost black.

I took a deep breath. 'Look, he's seventy-six. And he made this crazy promise to his late wife that he was going to follow her into the afterlife . . . It was a high school sweetheart love story. Like *The Notebook*. And you know, everyone is entitled to take their own lives . . . Most countries allow for that, you know. . .'

His lips turned into a very thin line.

'Your eyes' colour changed,' I offered, uselessly.

'So did you have sex with him?'

I lowered my eyes. 'Yes I did. Yesterday, finally I did.'

A look of disgust flashed over his face. 'Did you even enjoy it?'

'No, I did not. I had to put a blindfold on.'

Seth gave out a deep groan and pulled at his platinum hair. 'Aaargh, I was so hopeful!' He stood up and went around pacing the room, punching the air with his fists.

'What? Hopeful about what?' I furrowed my brows, perplexed by his reaction.

He went to one corner of the living room, underneath a taxidermied head of a bull, put his palm on the stone wall and sighed dramatically. 'I think I fell in love with you Cassie. Yes, I think I actually did. I don't know why, but your energy is so different . . . I thought that . . . You were special . . .'

'I do feel special around you,' I said. 'I usually don't.'

'I'm not sure how I feel about you now. This is too fucked up.'

I closed my eyes, my head started to throb. 'Look Seth, I don't expect you to understand. I just . . . Can we please just be friends? I don't want to deal with this right now.'

'How could you? How could you even entertain such an idea?'

'How could I not? What are you talking about—it's like . . . Ten million. I'll be retired in one year.'

'In exchange for what? *Your soul?*' He pulled his hair and paced around the room again, looking at me accusingly.

'My soul?' I laughed. 'Seth! I'm simply keeping him company . . . And helping him make good of his promise to his late wife . . . Yes sure, I won't ever have sex with him without this arrangement, but so what? Everyone has a price. Everything is transactional . . . After all . . . You have sex for all sorts of reasons—lust, greed . . . People marry each other for all sorts of monetary reasons . . .'

He looked like I just slapped him. 'Do you really think that . . . About . . . *love?*'

I was flustered. A part of me was angry that he was judging me so harshly, and another part of me wanted him to understand.

'Love? The kind that your parents have enjoyed, you mean? Is that the only acceptable form of love, for you? The only *good love* there is?'

'You are going to kill him, Cassie.'

'We don't know about that yet, okay. But if he needs any help, yes most likely we are going to assist—' I stopped halfway, thinking that I might have shared too much.

Seth was smiling now, almost ironically. 'So is that your price then, eh? Ten million dollars?'

'Sure.' I said, coldly. 'Everybody has a price.'

'No, not everyone. Not the love of my life, no she won't even dream to consider entering such an arrangement . . .'

'Oh please, stop making this all about you!' My voice rose in intensity. 'The love of your life? You are only in your mid-twenties! I never judged whatever you are doing with your life, whatever crypto scam you are scheming . . .'

'I'm not planning to kill anyone or have sex with an elderly I don't find attractive!'

'You really don't get me.'

'No, you're right. I don't.'

There was nothing much left to say. I was trembling like a leaf, I thought that I was going to be sick.

'I do really like you, you know that right . . . It's not . . . It's not a lie. You are truly special . . .' I told him, it sounded almost like a plea.

His eyes softened and brightened momentarily, his shoulders drooped. He walked slowly towards me, leaned over and kissed my forehead.

'You are too . . . Dark for me. Just too dark. Maybe you think this is stupid, but I still believe in Disney romance . . .'

To my horror I could feel tears streaming down my cheeks. I was not sure what I was crying about. I was not sure how to fix this, how to backtrack on my words, how to delay the inevitable.

'Hey, hey, *ssshh* . . . don't cry . . . hey, do you want to know a secret?' He kneeled in front of me and held my chin in his palms. 'My mom gave me this giraffe soft toy when I was a kid. I still sleep with him in my bed . . . Everyday. I'm that kind of a person, alright?'

It was too late now, I knew it was too late.

'This conversation never happened . . . I have never heard of this from you. I suggest we cease all forms of communication now . . . And if one day I watch the news, about an old man in Florida putting bullets in his brain . . . I'd try not to think of you . . .'

'Seth, please . . .'

'Sssshh,' He put his finger on my lips. 'I think it's about time that we go our separate ways. Would you like me to call you a cab?'

I had never felt lucky in love. My unrequited first love taught me that love was synonymous with unsatisfied longing. This was followed by a high school boyfriend who turned away from me with seemingly no second thought. Zaneta was precarious, unpredictable, and indecipherable. A string of hookups in and out of college, while fun and eye-opening, had made me feel incapable of being truly seen.

I held tight to that memory now, that moment Seth told me that he thought he fell in love with me, now I saw that as proof of a version of me that was unspoilt, untempered, worthy of love. I thought of what could have been, at which point in my life it had gone really wrong, yet I knew that some things must have been immanent, and I kept building on the architecture of my wounding, until it became wholly ingrown in the flesh of my being. Seth saw through the wound right away, yet it was still not enough to make him stay. He had far too healthy boundaries for that.

Everybody left.

My mother found out about my father's affair with Cinta in the fall of my high school senior year. I was surprised it took her so long, but perhaps she was just waiting for the right moment to speak her truth. I suspected she had been collecting evidence all along too, keeping trinkets, ticket stubs, receipts and lipstick-stained napkins, like a thousand little stabs, kept in boxes somewhere I could not even find. Or perhaps she was truly clueless all this time, or perhaps she chose not to see.

I believed it was an indisputable text message that gave him away, found blinking on his home screen—something that piqued my curiosity as well. How could he be so careless, after all those years, except if he actually wanted to be found out? The text message came from her, saying: 'Honey, ily. Last night was amazing. I can't wait to see you again, xx.'

At that time my parents were travelling together on a cruise trip in the Caribbean—Father went to the restroom and Mother was holding on to his phone. In the aftermath, as she recounted to us, she had collapsed onto the ground, her face turned white, her limbs icy.

What followed afterwards was a maelstrom of rage and tears that lasted for a decade and beyond. Glasses and curses were thrown liberally, violent screams from countless heated fights woke me and my sister in the middle of the night. She went over to Cinta's house and threw rocks at her window.

Since then, their power dynamic had tipped in her favour. Father was on his knees a lot, begging for her forgiveness, He was repentant, obliging, appeasing. She was contemptuous, blaming, temperamental.

I went to the United States shortly after, with a huge sense of relief—my last words to my mother before my departure was to please take the leap of faith and get a divorce. To my Father, I told him to please man up and support her if she chooses to go on her way. She never did leave him. She never truly healed either.

Mother went through a few more plastic surgeries in the years that followed—nose reconstruction and Botox, eyelids and face lifts. She rarely wanted to be photographed, and whenever that happened, she would heavily edit every single image before uploading it online. As she grew older, she grew increasingly bitter with how her life story had evolved and climaxed, and every little thing my father did would make her fly off the handle, even more so than before.

She begrudged us too—she could not help it—for we were the main reason she never forged her own path. However I knew that she would not have it any other way. She loved us too much to prioritize the love she had for herself. I wished I could have made her *see* that it was not possible to give love from an empty cup.

Sometimes it crossed my mind that it was a good thing that nobody ever loved me so and claimed me for life, so that nobody would ever betray me. I did not know if I could ever survive something like that.

The penthouse was empty again. It was around two in the afternoon. The cab Seth ordered and paid for dropped me off by the main entrance. I was more than distraught with how things had collapsed with Seth, but I was even more dreadful of facing Covert and Zaneta again. I did not know how to bring it up to them, but I might have to negotiate a platonic arrangement. Perhaps in exchange, I would volunteer to be the only one between us to pull the plug in the future. I did not know if this was the right move either. One thing I knew was that I had gone in too deep to turn back—I had crossed a point of no return, lost the first boy who ever truly loved me, and I could not walk away without that ten million dollars in my bank account.

Zaneta left a post-it on the table—*We are doing a grocery run, brb. Call me if you need us to get you anything.*

I felt tired, the whole ordeal back-to-back had sapped my energy and left me feeling empty and dry. I went to Covert's bedroom and lay on the soft mattress. I closed my eyes and fell into darkness within seconds.

I woke up with a gasp. Somehow I kept doing that, something about this place kept getting under my skin. I remembered dreaming about bones and bonfire again, but the more I tried to recall this figment of memory, the more it slipped away, like trying to hold a pool of water in my palm.

The clock showed 4:20 p.m. in the afternoon, but Covert and Zaneta remained nowhere to be seen. I sat up and looked around. I started feeling claustrophobic in this penthouse, spacious as it was. Covert's room was brightly lit from the floor-to-ceiling glass doors that opened to the wraparound balcony. The ocean reflected crystalline tiny dots in the distance. I thought that it was all too harsh, I was paralysed in the flood of brightness.

The string to the attic was winking persistently at the periphery of my vision, it felt almost unbearable. I walked over and yanked it down. It swung wildly above my head, but it did not budge. The key must be somewhere here, I thought to myself. I decided that I must find it, for there was nothing left to do here. I had the same kind of resolve as I had last time when I decided that I needed to collect proofs about my father's mistress.

I needed to know her, I needed to know Margaret—that was the only way that I would make the right decision in this situation. I felt surprised that I did not think of this sooner. I paced around the room, looked through the closet, underneath the bed, in the usual places of suspect—among the underwear, socks and belts. I went to the desk, checking all the drawers, flipping through stacks of postcards and crumpled grocery lists. I stopped to open the first page of Covert's notebook. It was his diary. I did not think that Covert was the type who would keep a journal.

For a moment I could barely decipher what he was writing— it was all too narrow and cursive. I squinted hard and saw that he wrote—

'Friday, 24th of April.

I don't want to die, please Margie. I cannot do this. Please, don't make me do it. I'm sorry. I'm really sorry.'

I flipped to the next page.

'Saturday, 25th of April.

I would do anything, what would you want me to do? I know there is no way I could make this up for you. Would you want me to build a mausoleum in your name, in Raleigh? Please Margie, don't do this to me.'

I realized that Covert was pleading to his late wife in his diary as if she were alive. My hair stood up on my arms. I read on. He talked to her every day, he told her his day-to-day routine—what he ate for breakfast and lunch and dinner, what he did the whole day. However, I did not see him writing about Zaneta.

I flipped pages after pages, I could not take my eyes off them. At times Covert was happy, endearing, sentimental. He missed her dearly and he could not wait to join her. At other times he was afraid, pathetic, miserable—he longed to be released from her underworld shackles. His moods swung widely, but one thing that I was sure of was that he talked to Margaret with sincere conviction, he was writing as if he could see her, clear as daylight.

'Monday, 7th of July.

You look beautiful today, Margie, more beautiful each day. I don't care what people say about knobbly knees and crow feet, I see that your eyes today are of wonderful shades of blue and green—they look mesmerizing. Margie, you do know that I have always seen into your soul, and this soul was far more beautiful than anything else in the world of flesh.'

In the December section, about eight months after Margaret's passing, I found a page that mentioned Zaneta. He was pleading and in tears.

'Saturday, 23rd of December.

Margie, Margie, how could I ever repent, how could I ever redeem what I had done to you? Dear, dear sweetheart, if only you knew how much I suffer day in and day out in the knowledge that I had done something I could never take back. The thing is dear, I had betrayed you, truly, it was out of my control. But dear, please forgive me, I have never met someone who made me feel more alive. No, no, it is not the same kind of love. It is not the same, incomparable, really. My love for you endured, it grew steady like a sequoia tree—however, this girl, this girl, Zaneta Cohen. She was all rainbow ice cream of different flavours, with chocolate sprinkles on top. I had never tasted anything like it— and, and I was addicted, love. That's all I could say.

And you were sick, honey, so very sick—do you remember that? You could not get out of the bed, there were tubes sticking through your nose and throat. You pissed and shat yourself, you barely could open your eyes. Margie, it broke my heart to see you like that, I cried every single day by your bedside.

Could you blame me then, that I came up with a plan that was more definitive, for the sake of both of us? Could you really blame me for not wanting to wait in prolonged uncertainty and anxiety? It was clear to me that there was only one way that would ensure optimum happiness for everyone. Did you see any other way at all?

No, Margie, please—no I did not mean that. I would rather have you by my side, truly, till the last moment. But Margie, no you were not by my side—you were not functioning Margie. I was not attended to, and I had my needs too . . . and Zaneta, dear, no, please don't hate her. She was truly a gift to me Margie, truly. She was like a stream of light by the end of the tunnel . . .

No, no, no Margie—please hear me out. No it's not like that. I would never, I would never . . . She meant well Margie. No Margie, don't do this to me, no. I'm sorry. I'm sorry. I'm sorry.

I'm sorry. I'm sorry. I'm sorry. I'm sorry. I'm sorry. I'm sorry. I'm sorry. I'm sorry . . .

. . . I'm sorry. I'm sorry. I'm sorry. I'm sorry. I'm sorry. I'm sorry. I'm sorry. I'm sorry. I'm sorry. I'm sorry. I'm sorry. I'm sorry. I'm sorry. I'm sorry.'

He wrote his apology non-stop for the next two pages. I found it horrifying, and something did not sit well in my stomach. I flipped to the last page, and there it was, pasted on the back cover of the notebook with cellophane tape—a tiny golden key.

I took it out, closed the notebook and placed it back on the table. I breathed in deeply to relax my nerves. I went to the vanity to get the chair, dragged and positioned it under the trap door. The golden padlock was still out of reach even with me standing on top of the chair, I tiptoed and stretched my arms as far as possible. I inserted the key into the padlock and turned it to the right. It opened with a click. I removed the padlock and placed it on the table with the key, next to Covert's notebook.

I pulled the string down, and the trap door fell, unleashing a retractable ladder. I pulled it out to its maximum length until it was secured stiffly on the carpeted floors. The stairs remained a little wobbly regardless, but I had to climb it. I balanced myself carefully on the bottom rung, and placed one foot on the second rung. Every time I hoisted myself up, I waited unmoving for a few seconds until the stairs balanced itself.

When I finally reached the top of the ladder, I poked my head into the pitch-black attic and started to scream.

Chapter Eleven

Unicorn and Fairy Tales on Her Grave

There was a body of a woman in the middle of the attic, lying unmoving on a single mattress. I could not move, I could not believe what I was seeing. 'Margaret . . .?' I whispered, just in case the body was alive.

After a few full minutes of staring on top of the ladder, I finally felt like I could move again. My fingers were ice cold, I swallowed hard several times to calm down my wildly thumping heart beat. 'Margaret?' I tried again. The body still did not respond.

I climbed up and stepped on the floor of the attic—the top of my head was touching the roof, I had to bend down a little. I inched forward, step by step. My limbs were trembling and heavy, but even in this state of shock, I observed how each footstep took an insanely tremendous amount of energy to expend. I thought about how this was another proof that our reality is relative, and everything is variable according to our mental perception.

I was finally by the side of the mattress. It was a hard and narrow mattress, covered in a plain, white cotton bedsheet. The body of Margaret was sleeping peacefully, fully supported. She was wearing a black, practical gown with long sleeves that extended until the top of her ankles. The body was gaunt, all bones and papery skin. Her withered hands peeked out from her sleeves and clasped together neatly on top of her stomach.

Her face, asleep and heavily made up in loose powder and blush. She even had purple shadows on her eyelids, her nails and her lips were painted in deep red. Her thick, auburn, hair spread like a halo of fans around her head—I wondered how it was preserved thick and colourful, it was probably a wig.

I extended my hand and touched her cheek. It was cold and dry.

Covert kept the embalmed body of his late wife in the attic of his summer penthouse.

I wondered if Zaneta knew—she must have known. Or perhaps this was even her idea. I could imagine her clapping her hands like a child. 'Oh Covert, let me do her make-up, let me, let me!'

I sniffed the air around Margaret. There was nothing foul—whatever he was doing with her, he took good care of this body. I was not sure if it was even legal to do this—but I should not be feeling anymore surprised at this point of time. Of course there was a body in the attic—how could I expect anything less?

The attic was clean and smelling faintly of pine leaves. I saw a treasure chest in the corner, a few coloured zafus thrown on the floor, and a wooden chair. There was a small rectangular window on the roof, through which the light came streaming down. The floor was well swept, well kept, there was no dust, no spider web. It was after all, not that kind of attic, except for the mummy in the middle of the room.

I walked towards the treasure chest and pried it open. There were articles of women's clothing inside—skirts, gowns, blouses and ruffled tops, underwear, socks, shawls, hats and various other accessories. I rummaged through a box of jewellry, crystal hair pins and jade combs. From the look of it, Margaret seemed to have been a rather high-spirited and artistic person, though not one who was bold and colourful like Zaneta. I saw a lot of light pastel colours, flowery patterns and heart-shaped items.

There was nothing professional or businesslike—she was clearly a housewife, someone being taken care of most of her life.

There was something stuck in the bottom corner of the treasure chest, underneath a collection of trinkets, keychains, nondescript hoops and rings. I kept digging, struggling, and extracted out a small leather pouch. It was brown and peeling off, fastened tightly with a drawstring. The leather material was so thick that I could not surmise what it possibly contained.

I pulled the drawstring loose and reached inside, feeling sharp little stones. I poured them out into my palm, scrutinizing how they gleamed like ivory chips under the skylight, and then it hit me. *These were human teeth.*

I screamed again.

My hand convulsed violently and the teeth fell and scattered across the attic floor, clattering and echoing one after another. That was the final straw. Everything, everywhere at once broke a whirlwind of chaos in my head—I could not take this anymore, I could not be any second longer in this place.

I looked at Margie lying on the bed, and I thought I saw her neck move a few degrees to the right, her sleeping face now tilted in my direction, reflecting the sunlight, a slight smile on her lips.

I screamed from the top of my lungs and scrambled towards the attic's rectangular opening. I had difficulty breathing, I was gasping for breath, and tears streamed hysterically down my cheeks without my control. *I cannot, I cannot do this anymore.* My limbs knocked the wooden chair very hard and it fell with a loud thud to the floor. I did not feel any pain, I was numb, I did not see anything in front of me.

With great difficulty I reached the retractable ladder and hopped maniacally to the ground from the second rung. Dull pain shot up my knees as I tumbled and rolled on the carpeted floor. I collected my breath, whimpering and panting hard.

I looked up at the ceiling, at the open rectangular hole, and suddenly two heads appeared in the field of my vision. Covert and Zaneta.

'Cassie. Cassie. Calm down,' I heard her raspy voice, low and tense.

Covert crouched down and tried to touch me. 'Hey, relax, sweetie. Do you need a hug . . .'

I screamed again and writhed wildly, kicking and punching in every direction. 'Get off me! Get off me! Get off you psychopath! I'm going to call the police!'

I thought that I kicked him in his stomach. I heard someone groan and retreat into the background. Now it was Zaneta who squatted down to meet my eyes. 'Cassie, stop. Cassie, breathe. It's not what you think it is.'

'There's a preserved body in the attic! Margaret is preserved in the attic!'

'*Sssh, sssh* . . . I know, I know. It's alright.'

'*You knew??*'

'Sweetheart, you should not be overreacting . . . Embalming our deceased loved ones is a perfectly acceptable and understandable human emotional response . . . If you think about it. I'm surprised they make it illegal here in the United States, for whatever reason,' she rolled her eyes.

I sat up and narrowed my eyes at her. She looked perfectly happy and at ease, exactly like the day I met her on that fateful night at Harvard Yard. 'Please, Cassie. We are not boring people. We embrace the unconventional. You should not be fussing over things like this . . .'

'You should not go in there in the first place—I knew it was going to be like this,' Covert grumbled. He went away and came back with a glass of water. Despite everything, I felt grateful for it. The cool water felt smooth and soothing as it passed down through my cramped throat. My pulse started to slow down, my vision calibrated back to normal, I was breathing again.

'How did you do it? How did you ship her body without anyone knowing?'

Covert shrugged. 'Well the funeral was in Raleigh, in our hometown . . . I tipped the undertaker to get her out after the whole ceremony was done and we put her body in the trunk of my van . . . I drove all the way down here . . . It really is not that hard.'

'Nor surprising,' Zaneta chimed in. I knew what she wanted to say, that I should stop overreacting, that I should get a good grip of myself.

'Speaking of which dear, we need to figure out how to transport Margie to my estate in Palm Springs, California . . . We are going to stay there for my final year . . .' Covert said. 'The cross-country drive will be such a long journey, I'm worried her body will not be able to withstand it . . .'

'Yes, we need to research a little bit on this. You should ask your undertaker friend . . . But my guess is we would need an airtight body bag?'

They began to discuss this important logistical planning as casually as if they were discussing how to travel with a baby. I realized then that they had been doing this for a while—travelling with her body wherever he went. That explained why he kept writing in his diary as if she were by his side.

'Why—why would you do this?' I asked, finding my voice again. 'I don't understand—like what's the goal of carrying her mummified body all over?'

They both turned their heads and looked at me, as if I was stupid.

'Why Cassie? Why, of course, so that I would not forget my promise!' Covert seemed aghast at the audacity of my questioning. 'It was not even a choice for me. Which part of it did you not get?'

'And don't forget, that they must be buried together, we have to make sure of that too. So it's a good thing to have her body handy with us,' Zaneta raised her brows, and then muttered under her breath. 'Damn, that would be another big thing we have to figure out . . .'

'Yes we should be buried in the same plot of land, in the same coffin in fact. I want to cuddle her in the afterlife.' Covert nodded.

'Isn't that just romantic,' Zaneta sighed and plopped herself on Covert's bed.

I was not sure that romantic was the right word to describe this whole thing.

'Look, Cassie, I'm sorry you found out this way. We were going to tell you, I promised,' Covert added. 'It was just not the right time, you were here just for a trial and frankly . . . from the way you were going about opening forbidden places and nosing around . . . You clearly do not obey the rules prescribed for you . . . I'm worried this would prove to be a challenge later . . .'

'I think I have the right to know every card on the table in order to make an informed decision,' I countered a little bit angrily. 'It's only fair. I need to know everything.'

'Don't worry Covert,' Zaneta interrupted. 'After we come to an agreement, we would make her sign a contract later. Everything will be in black and white, and if she breaks anything she has agreed to sign . . . she should be written off your will . . .'

'Sure thing' I stood up and moved closer to Zaneta. I smoothened my crumpled shorts. 'I have another question.'

'Yes sweetheart?'

'I read your diary,' I gestured at Covert. 'I read it, back-to-back. You were talking to Margie everyday.'

Covert was as red as a lobster, his lips disappearing into a thin line. However I continued, 'You were apologizing to her, profusely. You said that . . . you had taken the matter into your own hands and . . . And that you had taken a more definitive path, for the sake of the both of you, something that ensured 'optimum happiness' for everyone involved. What did you mean by that?'

They both stayed silent.

'You are not supposed to read anyone's diary . . .' Zaneta began.

What did you mean by that?' My voice rose higher, I was about to get hysterical again. 'I need to know. I need to hear it from you! I deserve to know the truth!'

Covert was looking at his shoes, as if fascinated by them. He cleared his throat several times, and then, in a very low voice, he said: 'I pulled the plug . . . I shut down her breathing machine . . .

'She was unsalvageable . . .' he went on. 'We all knew she could not survive for long. Her organs shut down one by one. It was . . . It was a torture to watch her like that. She told me to join her into the afterlife, and I gave my promise. But I did not know *when* it was going to happen.

And then I met Zaneta, and we were having so much fun, and the more I spent time with her, the more I wanted to try everything. I felt that I had been missing so much in life . . . And . . . and there was not much time left for me to do everything. I realized that meeting Zaneta was the beginning of everything, and I wanted to begin living this new life immediately, no matter how short it should last.

Tell me—did I really have any other choice? As long as she was lying paralysed on the bed, I would not be able to travel or do anything much—yes, we did go to Japan—just for a week. I could not bring anyone back home either, it would be disrespectful towards her. Keeping her alive was just delaying the inevitability of her passing, and *my eventual suicide*. It was just prolonging misery for everyone involved, trapping us all in a black box of pain and uncertainty.'

'You don't know that,' I whispered. 'Miracles happen all the time, she might have just survived.'

Covert was crying intensely now. 'I'm not a bad guy Cassie, I'm not. I'm just a normal person, and I just want to be happy.'

'Did you tell him to do this?' I turned to Zaneta. 'Did you tell him to end her life?'

'Yes, Cassie. I did.' Zaneta sat very straight and tilted her chin up, as if daring me to challenge her. 'That was the best move for everyone.'

I shook my head and went into Zaneta's room. I started refolding clothes in my suitcase and rearranging items. I packed my toiletries into the front pouch. 'What are you doing? You can't leave now,' Zaneta came behind me. I ignored her.

'If you were so convinced that you did nothing wrong, Covert, why would you apologize so in your journal?' I yelled from the bedroom, rolling socks into little balls and squeezing them at the corner of my flowing suitcase. 'Why would you beg her to forgive you? Stop lying to yourself. You knew that you did something *really* wrong.' I pressed the top of my suitcase shut and secured the padlock.

'And you . . .' I hissed at Zaneta. 'I'm not sure Zaneta. I'm not sure what to think of you now. I always thought you were just a little crazy, perhaps, yes, a little bit wild, someone who inspires me. But you, you have officially become a murderer now . . . And you are about to commit another one!'

She raised her hand and slapped me hard across my cheek. It stung like a hot flash and for a moment I was blinded. There were tears in the corner of her eyes now, but she did not say anything more.

I put my palm on my cheek, thinking to myself how far we had come, since that night when she saved me, when she took me under her wings. I thought about all the things that she had made me do, all the sneaking out, all the sexperiments, with or without her. Or perhaps, it was unfair to say so, she did not make me do anything, but she made me *want* to do things. It was a marvel, that someone really could change you permanently, like a hammer coming in and chipping away the surface of a stone wall. Although it was clearly a one-way street, I never had any impact on her.

'I want out,' I whispered. 'I can't do this anymore. I can't keep up with you anymore . . . I'm tired, Zaneta. I'm really tired.'

I took out my phone to access the landing page of Delta Air Lines and quickly ordered a one-way ticket back to Boston. The flight was leaving in four hours. I went back to the living room and held out my hand to Covert, 'I need your credit card.'

He passed it to me without any resistance. He looked defeated. I keyed in his numbers into the payment portal and transacted the purchase. 'Could you call Ali to pick me up? *Now?*

I was worried that Zaneta would go hysterical. I was worried she would scream at me, ban me from leaving, and hurt me more. I was worried she would *murder* me, to keep me silent. Yet she did not do any of those things. She looked exhausted for once, in fact, as exhausted as I was. Her forehead was crisscrossed with deep frowns, her jaw slackened, her shoulder drooped. For once, I thought that she looked old and ugly, and for once, I thought that she looked *human*. It dawned on me that she was nearing forty years old by now. She was a fully matured and developed woman who went around wearing butterfly wings and glitters on her face.

When Ali arrived outside the condominium building, I gathered my suitcase and my backpack and charged towards the elevator without hesitation.

'You should kill yourself already and get this over with,' I spat my parting words. I turned around and let the elevator doors close behind me.

The airport was bustling with people looking important with their suitcases. Neon tube light shone bright and harsh above my head, while everything else seemed to be following a slow-motion time lapse, as if underwater. A part of me thought that this must be a dream, yet here I was, clutching my glossy paper plane ticket with one hand, another hand on my suitcase, feeling shaken to the core.

Palm Beach International Airport looked sterile and boring, constructed out of clichéd big glass walls and unappealing gray tiled floors, partially covered in ugly coarse carpet. I went through the horrible customs questioning, where a burly officer found a way to triple check my identity and grab at me rudely. After what felt like eternity, I finally settled at a Starbucks coffee shop, ordering a matcha green latte with extra foam.

A lady's mechanical voice blared from the speaker. 'Greetings to passengers of Delta Air Lines. Passengers of Delta Air Lines D095, on your way to Boston, Massachusetts, now it is time for boarding. Greetings to passengers of Delta . . .'

I took a deep breath. I stood up and rolled my suitcase towards the departure gate.

Chapter Twelve

She Was Louise to My Thelma, She Was My Everything

Back at Harvard, things remained the same, nobody seemed to be aware of how I spent my last spring break in college. My senior roommate, Beverly raved about Cancun and beach parties with all the hot alpha males in swimming trunks.

Zaneta wired me a check of eight thousand dollars for the spring break ('minus Thursday and Friday' she wrote in the note). I bought Beverly frozen yogurt from my earnings, she was a little bit taken aback by my sudden generosity. I was known to be good with savings and stingy as hell.

'Well, well, what an unexpected surprise,' she squealed delightfully at her frozen yogurt—vanilla mint extra-large size. 'So … tell me about your spring break? Did you stay back in the dorm?'

'Yes I did,' I mumbled semi incoherently. 'I was taking cleaning jobs. That's where my money is from,' I added quickly, as if she'd know.

'What a productive spring break,' she applauded. 'Yeah, I heard Dorm Crew can be very lucrative. Hugo earned like over a thousand last summer.'

It was our last semester together and classes felt like a joke. Most of us only had electives left. I declared pass/fail for two of my subjects, which meant I did not really need to do all of my homework. I took a studio class titled *Interpreting Novel into Dance* and had a lot of fun choreographing moves based on my readings of Virginia Woolf and James Baldwin. *These different ways to body-roll here, they signify the five different undulating voices that make up 'The Waves' in Woolf's seminal work.*

'Your body rolls all look quite the same to me,' was Beverly's feedback. She was a ballet dancer. I made a point to alter these rolls even more, each separated by different degrees facing the audience.

I loved Harvard. I loved reading heavy theoretical texts and literature and conjuring up circumlocutory, pretentious papers with confusing vocabulary, papers that could have been rewritten with fifty per cent less words.

The rest of my semester passed in a blink of an eye. Spring came in full force, flowers bloomed in the yard—marshmallows of bright pink and glowing yellow, green leaves and green grass sprouted their bushy-shelves everywhere. The weather became wet, little showers poured several times daily, almost like someone was having fun with a little showerhead up there in the big blue sky.

I stopped talking to Zaneta completely. She tried to call me several times and left messages in my inbox for weeks and weeks, but I could not bring myself to open them. I closed my eyes, and I was back in the attic. Margaret's lips moved ever so slightly, her eyes opened and unseeing.

I thought that I could not possibly stay in the United States any longer, that I should just check out and go backpacking for a while after graduation, but I told my parents I accepted a marketing job for a Walgreens outlet in Palm Springs, California. They asked me about the benefits of the job. I told them I could get all Walgreens products for free, for the rest of my life. Obviously this could not be true for all Walgreens employees. My parents were happy with it, nonetheless.

They booked a flight to attend my graduation in May. My sister was not coming, as she was busy with her PhD defense in Singapore. A part of me felt raw and melancholic, at the thought of my older parents, booking a flight proudly to attend my Harvard graduation. A proud, respectable girl graduating from the best university in the world, on her way to chart a respectable career with great perks. I wondered how they would have felt if they had known the truth.

They would never find out, I decided. I would come up with something to explain why I got fired after a year and needed to return home.

I took a cab and picked them up at Logan International Airport. My dad looked shorter in America, his pepper-and-salt hair gleaming under the lamp. My mom was as beautiful as ever, with her botoxed cheeks and painted hair, she looked not a day older than thirty-five. 'You look very young, Mom,' I complimented her.

'Money does it sweetheart,' she said. 'Money, and good genes. And a little bit of luck!'

My parents stayed at the fancy Hilton Hotel in Back Bay because almost all the Air BnBs in town were fully booked for graduation season. It was always exceptionally crowded nearing the summer. We went shopping downtown, buying more clothes and shoes for my 'upcoming working life' that I did not actually need. Shopping and taking me out to the restaurants had been the way my parents showed their love for me.

'You are a big girl now Cassie,' my mom squeezed my shoulders proudly in front of the mirror of a Macy's changing room. 'If you put on my dress and my shoes and walk around with your father, people might very well mistake you for myself. I can't believe how fast you have grown.'

The day of the graduation started early, as early as 6 a.m. where we were expected to suit up with our robes and report to the chapel in the courtyard. Beverly told me the night before that a group of them were going to take acid to make the procession more interesting, and whether I would like to join. I said yes before even batting my eyelashes.

6 a.m. the next morning, all the graduates filled the big chapel in the middle of the yard, looking fresh and sharp in their robes and hats. An older matronly woman started speaking on the podium in the corner, she might be the Dean Provost of something related to the student affairs, and hers seemed to be the first of many speeches that were to follow that day. Beverly pulled me aside and gave me a small tab of white paper.

'What do I do with this?' I asked her.

'Just let it melt under your tongue,' she said.

In the beginning there was nothing, then slowly, slowly, things started to sway in my field of vision. The rows of black robes and hats interspersed with brick walls diffused like liquid paint before my eyes. Waves of nausea started to hit, I was not feeling well. 'Trust the process,' I could hear Bre's voice echo in the background. 'Trust the process'.

I suppressed the urge to puke and roll around on the floors, trying to will away the discomfort and nausea. After what felt like forever, I finally found the strength to stand up tall and all of sudden, I was awash in euphoria—no more nausea, no more hell. It was heaven alright.

Colours popped before my eyes—the sky never looked so bright and blue, the grass so green and yummy, the flowers— oh the flowers! They were living rainbows! Nothing, nothing else really mattered but my love for the universe and every single living vibrating being that beat their hearts in tandem with mine. Oh, what a marvellous time to be alive!

The rest of the day melted into the fringe of my consciousness. I couldn't care less what every dignified person was chirping about from the tall podium. We marched into a single line to the yard and took our seats at the Harvard yard. I thought how perfectly beautiful the weather was today and how lucky we were to have today of *all the days* for a happy graduation day.

People took turns delivering speeches, poetry recitation, chanting and singing on the stage. Different speakers from different ages and genders, different ethnic groups and different disciplines took turns to remind us how lucky we were to be Harvard graduates, to set forth into the world and finally created our own impact. They were telling us that the brightest graduates would not do just a 'good job' in the world but would strive to create opportunities for others 'less fortunate' than us.

I was not sure where my parents were. Family members were invited to sit through the whole ceremony at a different section in the yard. I had a feeling they skipped the full ceremony to go shopping and would show up later to take pictures with me in my ceremonial gown.

I stayed happy and euphoric for a few hours under the sun. It was difficult for me to do normal things, such as operating my smart phone or looking for a bathroom. Yet, I couldn't care less. I was feeling and embodying happiness, and that was the only thing that matters. Then the effects started fading away—colours become less pronounced, things stop swaying so deliciously. Breanna announced, 'I think our descent has started.'

I walked my descent as I walked across the stage. Someone obscurely white and male and older reached out to move the tassel on my hat from left to right. I felt a little bit giddy but managed to present a straight face. Beverly came right after me and she tripped on the stage. She apologized profusely, placing full blame on her heels. Nobody seemed to notice or report our little mischief, so I figured we got a pass for the day.

The ceremony ended with Oprah talking on the stage—again praising us and celebrating our luck and our opportunity to really make an impact on the world's stage. 'You are the chosen ones, never forget that. And when things are done and dusted, your ceremonial robes washed and returned, you will know in your heart that once a Harvard graduate, you will always be a Harvard graduate. Never ever forget that.'

What a heavy name to live up to.

Beverly elbowed me and rolled her eyes and started sniggering. I thought of Zaneta. I thought they both would get along really well, but my friendship with Zaneta had always been shrouded in secrecy. I preferred to keep her separate from my otherwise almost perfectly normal college life.

We snapped numerous pictures for the graduation, mostly in front of the Widener Library—me with the whole class, me with my housemates, me with the roommates including Beverly. Me with Becky, my ex-roommate. Then we dispersed and I looked around for my parents.

There they were, carrying predictable shopping bags from Newbury Street. I took a few pictures with them, they held me proudly in their arms. By that time, the acid effects had completely faded away and my teeth had felt funny, my tongue like ineffectual rubber inside my mouth. I asked my parents if they needed anything or if they wanted to see any historical buildings. They told me to smile more for the pictures—I looked half asleep.

After the ceremony my parents took me out to eat at an Italian restaurant in the South End. We sat down to a meal of spaghetti, juicy-red steak, steamed broccoli and cheesy bread in tomato soup. I wore an orange dress with an orange hat and a pearl necklace from my mother. Mother was wearing her designer blue gown, and Father was similarly decked in a designer suit. I ate everything voraciously—apparently the acid low left you ravenous.

They had their flight booked the next day, back to Indonesia. They asked me if I would need any help to move out. Who would be staying with me in Palm Springs? How was I going to get there?

'I have my flight ready,' I told them. 'And I found nice housing through Craigslist. I have video-called the landlord, she is older and she seems responsible and nice.'

I could tell that they felt sad to be leaving me, and that I was going to continue to stay in America, so far away from home. I was overwhelmed by a mixture of bittersweet emotions for my parents—for their cold, dysfunctional relationship, for their inability to connect with each other and with me in real, vulnerable ways, for their trying so hard showering me with gifts and promises of financial support.

It got increasingly difficult to fake my Walgreen job, which I described as a one-year rotational leadership trainee program, in which I would get to switch into different departments, from business to product development, from operations to marketing to publicity. After the end of one year, it would be decided whether I would stay on and which department I would help to manage. They were asking a bunch of questions, none of which I had answers to.

Have you seen the office, what is it like? I can't find any description of Walgreens' headquarter in Palm Springs, California—where exactly will you be working? Can we come and visit? I hope there will be nice amenities at your workplace. I hope your colleagues will be nice and you will get along just fine, have you met any of them?

'Relax Mom, Dad.' I said, exasperated. 'I am not a young girl anymore. You have to trust me. You can't possibly control everything.'

My mother launched into a tirade on how I failed to appreciate their love for me and that it was my responsibility to assuage their fear, at the very least. 'We are not even asking you to take care of us, only asking you to take care of yourself properly and therefore giving us some peace of mind . . .'

I assured them that they were welcome to visit me three months into my job and checked my condition for themselves, and that I would not shut them out from weekly updates of my progress. 'If I end up unhappy,' I said, 'I know I can always go back home to the two of you. Thanks for providing me with this security.'

This seemed to placate Mother for a fair bit. I thought to myself that I would come up with another excuse three months later down the road.

Mother reached out and rubbed my hand gently. 'We're proud of you Cassie, really we do. We are sorry if we have not said this enough.'

I smiled back at her, but my mind was uneasy. I wished I could tell her all the things and that she would still tell me all the same things.

Looking back at my time with Zaneta, I realized one thing, that she had never truly changed me as I thought she had, but rather I had never been truly Cassandra in the first place. I had never been the girl that I thought was myself, I was someone else, lying dormant under the pretense of a character more comprehensible, more manageable, coming alive only through snippets of dreams and daydreams, flitting and colourful like a buzz of static visions. Zaneta simply gave me permission to be myself, all along it was me—my unruly, unbridled, uncontainable, inherent, self. I was a force of nature and she recognized that. I was meant to exist at the margins of systems, to disrupt and wreak havoc in my wake. I did not need to pretend. With her, the static buzz achieved a more solid, more permanent, more enduring quality.

Seth did not understand this of me, he did not see the *whole* of me, that my pain, my darkness were equal parts of me as my light, my heart-softness, my delicate sensitivity.

I was really a girl who would dance around a bonfire, skinny dip into the ocean under the full moon, get penetrated by a stranger among the shelves of a public library. I was a girl who would contemplate killing a man for millions, who would pack her bags, storm out through the door, and hitchhike with the next car on the road, book a one-way flight to Mexico and never look back. I was a girl who would let her hair down, wild and bleached under the sun, her skin tan and her legs full of scratches from a mountain hike.

I thought I was in love with Zaneta, but really, I was in love with myself. And now that Zaneta was gone, I feared that I would soon forget how to be myself ever again.

After my parents left town, I went to the Harvard Bookstore and purchased a plastic brown globe. I set it down on the floor of my dorm room, almost completely vacated by now, except for a few clothing items still hanging from the rack and my toiletries in the bathroom.

I closed my eyes and gave the globe a spin. I pointed my finger and it stopped abruptly, wobbling a little on its base. I opened my eyes.

That's where I'd start then. Greece.

Chapter Thirteen

The American Dream

I was lying on my back in the warm Laconian sea. The sky above looked maddeningly blue, deep and brazen like an infinite expanse of fabric stretched taut over a half-globe of water. There were no clouds as far as I could see, only solid blue and a round shining sun far above.

I made a circular movement with my arms around my head like a halo. The water was warm and unusually calm for an ocean, it almost felt like I could fall asleep easily, supported by its softness. Skin to molecules. The sun rays on my face.

There was a bluish gray and green mountain to the right in the horizon, looking so majestic that it must have risen from Atlantis itself. A rock castle perched on top of its slopes, now opened to the public as a hotel. I lived in that hotel.

I had no idea that summer days were made for crushed berries—and—butter sandwiches picnics, taking long walks into the olive groves to catch sunsets, and swimming bare breasts in empty oceans.

After graduation, I booked a one-way flight to Athens, on a special three-year European student visa that was granted from an exchange program I did with Aarhus University in my junior year. From Athens, I took a twelve-hour bus ride down south, to Cape Tainaron, the southernmost point of Greece and the whole of Europe. There were olive groves everywhere I saw and rows and rows of mountains stretching into the horizon. The sun was strong, almost brutal, but I appreciated how it burnt my skin golden brown.

The main attraction at Cape Tainaron was the ruins of an underground cave by a sparkling crystal-blue sea, that according to the legend was the remnants of Hades' portal to the underworld. About three kilometres walking distance from this cave, a lighthouse stood on top of the southernmost peninsula of Europe. Travellers came to take pictures at the cave and the lighthouse and swim in the warm ocean. They hung out at a handful of tavernas in the area for strong coffees, lamb chops, potatoes and wild greens.

I checked in at a cheap backpacker hostel my first night but started walking around to see what else I could do. It was not that hard to get a job. The castle hotel was restored from the 18th century, and it offered boutique accommodation at a slightly higher price than other guest houses in the area. I walked into the reception and told them that I was looking for a job.

They gave me kitchen cleaning duties and waitressing shifts in their in-house restaurant. I was paid five euros per hour, and given a bunk bed in the staff dormitory, a renovated building from what previously had been a stable for livestock.

In the mornings I woke up to watch the sunrise from the rooftop of the castle. After my shift ended, I would take a walk, read a book, or write something in my journal. I preferred to swim in the ocean close to sunset, around 9 p.m. in the evening. Every single day I saw riots of blue, pink, and purple faded slowly into dark velvet blue, dotted with glittery stars and a gentle white moon. It never got old.

I started penning my thoughts on paper. I wrote a few lines here and there, things that might shape up into the beginning of a novel, a story that came alive from the recesses of my memory.

The Suicide Pact of The Very Rich Man

~~Once upon a time, there were two girls who became best friends..~~

Once upon a time, there was a very rich man who wished to die. He hired two girls, one blonde, one raven, to first keep him company, and then to help him take his life. ~~He contemplated carbon monoxide poisoning, ingesting cyanide, hanging with a rope from the ceiling.~~

Once upon a time, there was a shy girl, who stumbled into the most outrageous sugar dating proposition in the world.

It had been very difficult to start, somehow I could not get past even one full page. I tore down and crumpled pages after pages that filled up the trash can in my dorm room.

Before I knew it, one month had passed, and then two months. I worked about five hours daily, Monday to Saturday, keeping to the flow of serving coffees and scribbling in my notepad. On Sundays I would hitch car rides with other staff to explore other beaches, mountains, rivers and waterfalls in the Peloponnese region. Time was moving very quickly and simultaneously in a standstill, warped almost permanently in the world that I was living.

Close to the end of my fourth month living in Greece, as summer started to give way to the fall season, a letter from Zaneta arrived, addressed to the receptionist of the castle hotel.

The envelope was bright pink, with red heart and blue cloud stickers pasted liberally all over. I knew it was her even before I opened it. I waited until lunch time to sit down properly at one of the tables of the restaurant before tearing the envelope. Her handwriting did not change, it was big and curly, with over-flourish at the top and the bottom of the letters.

My dearest Cassandra,

I trust that this letter finds you well. Please do not be alarmed, for I have taken the liberty to hire a private investigator to track your whereabouts. You have changed your mobile number and blocked me completely out of your life. There's nothing left I could do to reach you.

While I respect your decisions, my heart is breaking every day at the thought that you hate me so. Dearest Cassie, my sweet little Cassie, I hope you don't blame me for the way you have grown and transformed in the past four years. I hope that you would be proud of your experiences, your boldness, your appetite to live an extraordinary life.

At the moment I am writing to you from Edinburgh, I just started a PhD program here last month, and I do not know quite clearly what to think or how to feel. Things had fallen apart with both Blake and Covert and turned upside down almost overnight. I am still absorbing the shocks of recent events.

Blake had undergone an ECT therapy for his depression, and somehow started having amnesia. He claimed to not have remembered me anymore, our memories, or our engagement. He was a different person altogether. He remembered his thesis, his studies, and his paper, but it appeared that his personal relationships had been completely erased from his conscious waking memory.

He packed his bags and moved out of our place. He apologized for having forgotten about me, but he told me that he could not force himself to be in love with a stranger. I was crushed, I lost all motivation to do anything. I could not handle Covert anymore. I told him that I needed to get away.

Covert gave me a lump sum of money, not the amount that we discussed, but substantial enough for me to be able to not work for decades perhaps. He told me that it was only fair, as I had kept him entertained for a little bit more than two years. I had not talked to him since July but the last thing he told me was that he moved back to his apartment in New York City to be closer to some of Margaret's artist friends.

I have taken the liberty to track your whereabouts because I want to gift this to you, with Covert's blessings. He told me to share some with you, and I knew that he had given Bonnie a lump sum amount as well. I decided to give this amount to you not just for what happened during the spring break, but as a token of appreciation for our friendship.

Dearest Cassie, as you must have known, I am not making this up. I never made things up. My life, for better or worse, has always turned out to be more dramatic than the average person, and I am not sure why or how that this is the life that I am living. But I will not have it any other way.

I wish that you know just how much I treasure our friendship, and how highly I think of you. You are the sweet one, the sensible one, yet you light fires from within, and in your power, you stand up tall and strong.

If I think back to the day that you stormed off the penthouse in Florida without hesitation, now I see that you had done right by us. It was not right, what we were trying to do, no matter how much our logical brains would justify it. Anyone alive and healthy should not entertain the thought of killing oneself. I'm sorry for even proposing such an arrangement in the first place, and for knowingly manipulating your soft spot for my every whim and request.

I'm sorry. I hope you will forgive me one day. I love you.

With all my heart,   .
Zaneta Cohen

In the envelope was a cheque for five hundred thousand US Dollars, paid in full to Cassandra Lie Setiawan. I could not think straight. For a moment I thought that my ears were buzzing with white noise.

I am half-a-million dollars richer today, I said it aloud in my mind.

I could buy a house, maybe a car, maybe a second-hand yacht, and sail around the world without care for a number of years. My happy-ending was finally here, unexpectedly, it fell straight onto my lap like a surprise gift from heaven. Yet I felt nothing but jaded, almost broken-hearted.

That night, I called Covert on WhatsApp. I sneaked out of my dormitory room and climbed to the hotel's rooftop to sit under the moonlight. I still had his number saved in my phone, and his WhatsApp showed that he was active recently. He had an old photograph of himself and Margie as the profile picture, he was hugging her from behind, all big smiles and white teeth.

He answered on the third ring.

'Huh? Who's this?'

'Hey Covert. Remember me? It's Cassie here.'

Silence for a while, I heard statics through the phone line. I was afraid that he might hang up.

'Cassie . . . ah yes . . . how are you . . . How are you dear?'

'I'm good,' I said. 'I'm in Greece right now. Zaneta just sent me a cheque of five hundred thousand dollars. I thought I should say thank you.'

Silence again.

'Thank *her*, don't thank me,' he answered. 'But yes, I figure I'd better give most of it away, while I'm still alive. I thought about it, we could not have pulled it off anyway. The police will be suspicious about where my money goes after my passing . . .'

'I figured so too.'

'How are you doing anyway?' I asked, almost like an afterthought.

'I'm not good, to be frank. Not good at all . . .'

'Why? Because Zaneta left?'

'Yeah—that too I suppose. But the fact of the matter is . . . I'm dying now Cassie . . . Dying for real.'

'You are?'

'Yeah, I'm staying in my apartment in Manhattan now . . . Doctor just told me. I have stomach cancer. I have been having stomach pains for a while . . . but I thought it was nothing. He said I only have about two months to live.'

'That's horrible!' I yelped, and sincerely so. I was surprised at how emotional I got, hearing this, after entertaining the thought of killing him myself. 'Well . . . Isn't that what you want, then? The universe takes care of it for you.'

'That's the funny thing Cassie . . . I really, really don't want to die,' His voice was trembling now. 'All this time I thought I was healthy and that my life was my own to take away, but now I feel powerless, like I do not have any other choice. And really, I don't want to go yet. I just don't want to.'

'I'm sorry to hear that, Covert,' I did not know what else to say.

'I still feel guilty every day,' He continued. 'And now even more so. I feel guilty towards Margie, for taking her life. And I feel guilty for not being able to take my own life as I had promised her. I am a useless, useless man. And now I am about to die. I am living in literal hell.'

He started sobbing now, hiccupping and gasping for breath. I held the phone close to my ear and let him cry. There was nothing much left to say.

'I am writing a book now,' I told him finally. 'About us. About you and Margaret. It is fiction.'

'When it's done,' I went on, 'I'll send a copy for you.' I did not have the heart to add that he might be gone when it was done.

He stopped sobbing, and for a full minute everything was quiet again.

'Write well for me, would ya?'

His parting words at last.

'Write well for me, for Margie, and for Princess. Make all of us proud. And let it be my last legacy on earth.'

Epilogue

The American Dream—dreamy people, dreamy places on the pages of bright glossy magazines. Their tailored suits and dresses and wide straw hats, their teeth seemed so white, their skin so tan from their summer vacations in The Hamptons. White picket fenced polly-pocket houses made out of clapboards painted in white and pastel colours. Fresh, green, lawn mown to perfection, with pink, red, yellow, and white roses bloomed in the background. There was a car in the driveway, a beige glossy sedan, big enough for a family of four.

The American Dream—celebrities and A-listers, tech moguls and superstars, gracing the front pages of the very same glossy magazines. People there seemed to have it all—money, status, influence, power. They must have eaten the best of food, had the best of parties, had the best of sex.

The American Dream was this infinite knowing that everything was possible, that imagination was our only limit, that every other day in America you could win a lottery ticket. If you made it in America, you made it everywhere else in the world.

And then there was Harvard. OH THE GRAVITY of the damned title, equal part a blessing equal part a curse. The expectation that *you've got to* make something out of your one precious and talented life. I had to be honest, sometimes I spent my days waiting for when the promised dream life would befall me, a dream life fitting only for those on the front pages of all the glossy magazines. Salaried work was not enough, white collar workers were far too mundane. I had to be a part of something grand, something wild and exciting and unapologetically extraordinary.

As I grew older though, and my time at Harvard had finally become a distant memory, and I slowly, excruciatingly, *finally* settled into my adult skin, I realized that none of it had truly mattered. Harvard was a possibility, people on the glossy magazines were a possibility, wealth, fame, and glory were a possibility, a happily ever after was a possibility, but a dream remained a dream.

What I had, what mattered, undisputedly so, was only today. So today I rose, today I tried again, and today I lived like there was no tomorrow.